Arthur Alger Crozier

The Cauliflower

Arthur Alger Crozier

The Cauliflower

ISBN/EAN: 9783337106645

Printed in Europe, USA, Canada, Australia, Japan

Cover: Foto ©Andreas Hilbeck / pixelio.de

More available books at **www.hansebooks.com**

EARLY ALABASTER.—(SEE PAGE 127).

THE
CAULIFLOWER

BY

A. A. CROZIER.

ANN-ARBOR, MICHIGAN:
REGISTER PUBLISHING COMPANY,
The Inland Press.
1891

CONTENTS.

INTRODUCTION.

The cauliflower is one of the minor vegetables which is now attracting more than ordinary attention in this country, and being grown with remarkable success and profit in a few localities which have been found to be particularly adapted to it. With most of our gardeners, however, it is still considered a very uncertain and unprofitable crop. This is due not only to the peculiar requirements of the cauliflower as to soil and climate, but also to the want of familiarity on the part of most American gardeners with modern varieties and with methods of cultivation adapted to our climate.

For a number of years, while engaged in market gardening and fruit growing in Western Michigan, the writer made a specialty of raising cauliflowers for the Grand Rapids and Chicago markets, planting from three to five acres a year. During this time most of the varieties offered by American seedsmen were tested, and the best methods of cultivation sought. On the whole, the cauliflower crop was found more profitable than any other, with the possible exception of peaches. There were partial failures, but these were due to causes which might have been foreseen and prevented. The experience gained at that time, and subsequent observation, have convinced the author that there are many parts of the country in which the climate and soil are adapted to this vegetable, but where its cultivation is yet practically unknown. The requirements for success with cauliflower will be found to be simple but imperative. A few direct experiments may be needed after one has gained the general information herein set forth, to enable one to determine whether it is best to continue or abandon its cultivation in his own locality.

I have endeavored to treat the subject in a manner adapted to the diversity of conditions found within the limits of the United States. With no vegetable is it more important to have fixed rules for one's guidance than with the cauliflower; but these rules must of necessity be of the most restricted application; in fact, they require to be adjusted to almost each individual case. So, while I have not omitted to give minute, practical directions where they seemed necessary, I have endeavored to call attention to the circumstances under which they are to be employed, and must here caution the grower against following them too implicitly under different circumstances. This remark applies particularly to the selection of varieties and the dates of planting.

Under the head of " Management of the Crop" will be found the most important information of general application, while in the chapter on " Cauli-flower Regions" are given numerous records of experience from growers in all parts of the country, which will be found of special value for each locality.

Those who desire direct information on particular points will consult the index and turn at once to the paragraphs which treat of soil, culture, enemies, marketing, best varieties, etc. It is unfortunate that confusion exists in regard to some of the varieties, but it seemed best to make the list as complete as possible, even at the risk of introducing a few errors. The confusion (which is more apparent than real), arises, in part, from seeds of certain varieties having been sold at times for those of others, and in part from the extreme liability of the varieties of the cauliflower to deteriorate or change. Errors from both these sources, when reduced to a minimum by the accumulation of evidence, reveal the fact that there are varieties and groups of varieties which have acquired well defined characters, and that the differences between the varieties are increasing rather than otherwise as time goes on. The selection of varieties for planting is a matter to be determined largely by the locality where they are to be grown. The differences between them lie mainly in their adaptation to particular purposes. There are almost none but what are good somewhere.

I cannot omit to emphasize here the fact that the fall crop should be mainly relied upon in this country. It is a waste of time to attempt to have cauliflowers head in our hot summer months, and until our markets are better supplied than they now are with this vegetable, it will not often pay to do much with the spring crop. The time may come when, as in England, we may expect to have cauliflower and broccoli the year round, but it has not come yet.

The chapter on cooking cauliflower should not be overlooked. One reason why there is such a limted demand for this vegetable in this country is that so few here know how to cook it. The methods of cooking it are simple enough, but there are many persons who always hesitate to try anything new, and as cauliflowers do not appear regularly in the market these people never learn how to use them.

Those interested in extending the market for this vegetable will do well to devise special means for introducing it into families not familiar with it. The writer found that foreigners who had been accustomed to the use of cauliflower in the "Old Country" were his best customers.

THE CAULIFLOWER.

CHAPTER I.

ORIGIN AND HISTORY.

On the sea-coasts of Great Britain and other countries of western Europe, from Norway around to the northern shores of the Mediterranean (where it is chiefly at home) grows a small biennial plant, looking somewhat like a mustard or half-grown cabbage. This is the wild cabbage, *Brassica oleracea*, from which our cultivated cabbages originated. It is entirely destitute of a head, but has rather succulent stems and leaves, and has been used more or less for food from the earliest historic times. The cultivated plants which most resemble this wild species, are our different sorts of kale. In fact this wild plant is the original, not only of our headed cabbage in its different varieties, but also of all forms of kale, the kohl-rabi, brussels-sprouts, broccolis and cauliflowers. No more wonderful example than this exists of the changes produced in a wild plant by cultivation. Just when the improvement of the wild cabbage began is unknown, probably at least 4000 years ago. Of the cultivated forms of this species Theophrastus distinguished three, Pliny, six; Tournefort, twenty; and De Candolle, in 1821, more than thirty. For a long time this plant was used for food in a slightly improved state before heads of any kind were developed. Sturtevant, quotes Oliver de Serres, as saying that, "White cabbages came from the north, and the art of making them head was unknown in the time of Charlemagne." He adds that the first unmistakable reference to our headed cabbage that he finds is by Rullius, who in 1536 mentions globular heads, a foot and a half in diameter. It was probably about this time that the cauliflower, and several other forms of the species made their appearance. There is difference of opinion as to whether our cauliflowers or the broccolis were first to originate. Loudon believed that the broccolis, which Miller says first came to England from Italy in 1719, were derived from the cauliflower. Phillips, in his "History of Cultivated Vegetables," said, in 1822, that the broccoli appears to be an accidental mixture of the common cabbage and the cauliflower, but of this he gives no proof.

Sturtevant says: "It is certainly very curious that the early botanists did not describe or figure the broccoli. The omission is only explainable on the supposition that it was confounded with the cauliflower, just as Linnæus brought the cauliflower and the broccoli into one botanical variety." When broccolis came to England from Italy, they were at first known under the names "sprout-cauliflower," or "Italian asparagus." This, however, is not sufficient reason for believing that the broccolis are derived from the cauliflowers, as the word broccoli was, and still is, applied in Italy to the tender shoots of various kinds of cabbages and turnips.

Some recent authorities have believed, since the broccoli is coarser than the cauliflower, more variable in character, more robust in habit, and requires a longer season, that it is the original form, of which the cauliflower is only an improvement. Thus, Vilmorin says: "The sprouting or asparagus broccoli represents the the first form exhibited by the new vegetable when it ceased to be the earliest cabbage, and was grown with an especial view to its shoots; after this, by continued selection and successive improvements, varieties were obtained which produced a compact white head, and some of these varieties were still further improved into kinds which are sufficiently early to commence and complete their entire growth in the course of the same year; these last named kinds are now known by the name of cauliflowers."

At the Cirencester Agricultural College, England, about 1860, broccolis were produced, with other variables, directly from seeds of the wild cabbage. These, and other considerations, make it seem doubtful that our broccolis have originated from our cauliflowers. Whatever the original form of the cauliflower may have been, it seems more probable that the broccolis now grown had a separate origin, either from the wild state or from some form of kale. Nearly all our present varieties of broccoli originated in England from a few sorts introduced from Italy.

Cauliflowers, in name at least, are older than the broccolis, and were brought to a high state of development and widely distributed before the latter are mentioned in history. They were grown in the Mediterranean region long before they became known in other parts of Europe.

Sturtevant finds no mention of the cauliflower or broccoli in ancient authors, the only indication of the kind being the use of the word *cyma* by Pliny for a form of the cabbage tribe, which he thinks may have been the broccoli. Heuze states that three varieties of cauliflower were known in Spain in the twelfth century. In 1565 the cauliflower is reported as being extensively grown in Hayti in the New World.

In 1573–5, Rauwolf, while traveling in the East, found the cauliflower cultivated at Aleppo, in Turkey.

It seems to have been introduced into England from the Island of Cypress, and it is mentioned by Lyte, in 1586, under the name of "Cypress coleworts."

Alpinus, in his work on the "Plants of Egypt," published in 1591, states that the only plants of the cabbage tribe which he saw in that country were the cauliflower and kohl-rabi. Cauliflower was also well known in Greece at an early day.

Gerard published a figure of it in England in 1597. In 1612 it is reported as being cultivated in France, and in 1619 as being sold in the London market. In 1694 Pompes, a French author, is quoted as saying that, "It comes to us in Paris by way of Marseilles from the Isle of Cypress, which is the only place I know of where it seeds."

From this time on, its cultivation gradually extended throughout Europe. In England, especially, the cauliflower, as well as the broccoli became a popular garden vegetable. Philip Miller, in his "Gardener's Dictionary," published in 1741, gives a long description of the method of growing this vegetable, though mentioning but one variety, while several varieties of broccoli are described. He says, however, that "cauliflowers have of late years been so far improved in England as to far exceed in goodness and magnitude what are produced in most parts of Europe." Prior to the French Revolution, (which began in 1788,) cauliflower had, in fact, come to be largely exported from England into Holland, Germany and France; but soon after this it came to be more generally grown in those countries and was no longer imported, though English seed was still used.

The numerous varieties of cauliflower now cultivated are of comparatively recent origin.   Although some of the earliest writers on this vegetable mention two or more varieties, these were in some cases merely different crops produced by sowing the seed at different periods.   In 1796, Marshall, in his English work on gardening, says that "cauliflower is sometimes distinguished into an early and late sort; though in fact there is no difference, only as the seed of that called 'early' is saved from the foremost plants."   Phillips, in 1822, said: "Our gardeners furnish us with an early and a late variety, both of which are much esteemed."

In 1831, Don, of England, in his work on botany and gardening ("History of Dichlamydeous Plants") describes fifteen varieties of broccolis and three of cauliflowers.   The latter were known as Early, Later or Large, and Red, the last being the most hardy.   These three kinds differed but little in general character and were all inclined to sport into inferior varieties.

In 1832 there was still a discussion in England as to whether the early and late cauliflowers were really distinct, or differed only in time of sowing.

John Rogers, in his "Vegetable Cultivator" (London, 1843), said: "There are two varieties of the cauliflower, the early and the late, which are alike in their growth and size, only that the early kind, as the name implies, comes in about a week before the other, provided the true sort has been obtained. There is, however, no certainty of knowing this, unless by sowing the seed from the earliest sorts, as is the practice of the London kitchen gardeners. The early variety was grown for a number of years in the grounds called the Meat-house Gardens, at Millbank, near Chelsea, and was of a superior quality, and generally the first at market. The late variety is supposed to have originated from a stock for many years cultivated on a piece of ground called the Jamaica level, near Deptford, and which produced uncommonly fine heads, but later than those at Millbank. Both soils are nearly similar, being a deep rich loam, on a moist subsoil, and continually enriched with dung. Both the varieties are of a delicate nature, being generally too tender to resist the cold of the winter season without the occasional aid of glasses or other means; and the sight of many acres overspread with such glasses in the vicinity of London gives a stranger a forcible idea of the riches and luxury of the capital."

In France, in 1824, three varieties, differing mainly in earliness, were recognized, *le dur*, *le demi-dur* and *le tendre.* These names are still applied to well known French sorts.

Victor Paquet, in his *Plantes Potagers,* published at Paris in 1846, says: "The greater number of varieties of cauliflower are white, but some are green or reddish. They are cooked in water, and dressed with oil or white sauce. We cultivate two distinct varieties, *tendre* and *demi-dur.* The sub-varieties *gros* and *petit Solomon* are sorts of the *tendre.*"

Thus we see that early in the present century there were sorts differing at least in time of maturity which had originated by selection; and, although history does not show it, we must infer that even then there were distinct differences in the cauliflowers cultivated in different parts of Europe. From this time on cauliflowers from various localities were brought more into public notice and greater efforts were made toward their improvement.

In 1845, C. M. Hovey, of Boston, said, that "the varieties of cauliflower have been greatly improved within a few years, and now not less than a dozen kinds are found in the catalogues." The most noted of those mentioned by him are Walcheren and Large Asiatic—varieties still in cultivation. Burr described ten sorts in 1863, and Vilmorin sixteen sorts in 1883. There are recorded in the present work the names of one hundred and forty varieties besides synonyms. Some of these varieties are no longer cultivated, and a few are too near other sorts to be considered worthy of a separate name; so that of the cauliflowers proper there may be said to be now in cultivation about one hundred distinct varieties.

CHAPTER II.

THE CAULIFLOWER INDUSTRY.

In the United States, as already stated, the cauliflower industry is but little developed. This vegetable receives, for example, far less attention than is given to celery, though it is more easily grown. One may look over the recent files of some of our agricultural and horticultural papers for several years together and not find the cauliflower mentioned. In fact, more general attention was given the cauliflower in this country forty years ago than to-day. The disappointments of those who attempted to grow cauliflower at an early day, expecting to grow it, as in Europe, with as little trouble as cabbage, have led to an almost universal belief that the cauliflower is peculiarly unreliable in the United States. This, for a large portion of the country, is true; but it is beginning to be known that there are localities where, with proper management, it is almost as safe as any crop.

It is by no means true that in Europe the cauliflower is everywhere grown with success. There are comparatively small areas, even in the most favorable portions of that continent, where it can be profitably grown. Although the climate of

Europe, as a whole, is better for this vegetable than that of the United States, the greater success with the cauliflower there is due largely to the greater care exercised in choosing proper soil, in fertilization, and in irrigation. The area of cauliflower growing has largely increased in Europe within the past few years. In the vicinity of Angiers, France, the growing of cauliflower for market began about 1880. In a short time it reached an extent of several thousand hectares (a hectare is two and one-half acres). There is found in this region a loamy soil, such as is especially suitable for this vegetable. The land is thrown up into beds twenty-five or thirty feet wide, with ditches between for irrigation. The rows are placed two and one-half feet apart, and the plants one and one-half feet apart in the rows. On the approach of winter the plants which are still unheaded are ridged up with earth for protection in the same manner as celery. The crop fails from too cold or too wet weather, about one year in five. The heads are mostly sent to Paris, and sell there at from forty cents to $1 per dozen. Even at these rates the crop is a profitable one, often bringing $300 per acre after paying the cost of marketing. Land is worth from $24 to $40 per acre. For three or four weeks in spring there are sent from Angiers to Paris, on an average, forty car-loads per day. In the immediate vicinity of Paris large quantities of cauliflower are grown for market.

In some parts of Germany the cauliflower is a very popular crop. Around Erfurt, which is nearly in the center of the empire, greater care is taken with its cultivation than probably anywhere else in the world, and large quantities are grown for seed. The late James Vick has told (Report Mich. Pom. Soc., 1874, p. 206,) how the low swampy land around Erfurt is thrown up into wide beds with ditches between, from which, every dry day, the water is dipped upon the plants. In Austria, also, cauliflower is a well-known vegetable, and several valuable varieties have originated in that country. Few seedsmen offer a more complete list of varieties than those of Vienna. In Italy the cauliflower has long been known, and in some places is a staple food of the poorer classes. Most of our standard late varieties are of Italian origin.

In Holland, cauliflowers are grown not only for home use and for seed, but also for the early London market. Around London the cauliflower has been extensively grown for a longer time than anywhere else, and it is there regarded as one of the most important garden crops. A recent English writer says: "With the exception of the potato, I question whether there is another vegetable to be compared with the cauliflower for general usefulness." Hundreds of acres are devoted to it near London, a large portion being under glass for the early crop. Formerly the cauliflower crop was all cut and sent to market, with the exception of a small portion saved for seed; but of late, extensive fields are purchased entire by Crosse and Blackwell for pickling purposes.

In the United States there are a few points where the growing of cauliflower for market is assuming considerable importance. On Long Island, in 1879, the crop was estimated by Oemler at 100,000 pounds, besides what was used for pickling. In 1885 Brill estimated the total crop of Suffolk County at about 125,000 barrels. In 1889, the value of the crop sold from Suffolk County was estimated at $200,-000, nine-tenths of all the cauliflowers sent to the New York market being grown in that county. At Farmingdale and Central Park, in 1888, two pickle factories used five hundred barrels of cauliflowers, besides the usual proportion of other vegetables. Much of the crop from Long Island is now sent to markets beyond New York. Philadelphia receives but little good cauliflower except that which comes from Long Island. The same is true of the city of Washington. The receipts in the latter city from Long Island for the three fall months of 1890 were about 20,000 barrels.

The Chicago market is seldom fully supplied

with cauliflowers and the price there averages fully as good as anywhere in the country. Considerable amounts are grown near the city, and small quantities are shipped in from Michigan, Wisconsin, Central Illinois, and even from California. One pickle factory at Crystal Lake, near Chicago, contracted, in 1874. for 16 acres of cauliflowers, besides other produce. The pickle factories always furnish a market for any surplus when the price is low, or the heads have become disfigured in any way. In fact. the supply of home grown cauliflowers is always insufficient for pickling purposes, and large amounts have to be annually imported, notwithstanding the tariff, which, formerly ten per cent., ad valorum, is now forty-five per cent. Imported cauliflowers are brought mainly from Germany and Holland, and come packed in brine in 60 gallon casks. Large quantities of mixed pickles containing cauliflower are also imported.

CHAPTER III.

MANAGEMENT OF THE CROP.

SOIL.

Almost any soil will do for the cauliflower, providing it is moist and fertile. The requirements of this vegetable as to soil are practically the same as those for the cabbage, except, that as the cauliflower will stand less drouth, it should generally have a heavier and richer soil, and rather more room. A soil which produces cabbages with large and rather soft heads is likely to be good for cauliflowers; that is, it contains more vegetable matter than the right amount for producing hard heads of cabbage. Muck will answer for cauliflowers if it is not too wet or too dry; it should like any other soil be treated to a good coat of barn-yard manure—horse manure being preferable on such land, as it promotes fermentation. Small quantities of lime may also be applied for the same reason.

The best soil is generally a strong sandy loam. Light sand or gravel is the poorest; and unless made very rich and artificially watered, it is useless to attempt to grow cauliflowers on such a soil in ordinary seasons. Heavy clay is less suitable for cauliflower than for cabbage, chiefly because on

2

such a soil the plants are apt to be small and late. In a warm climate a heavier soil is required than in a cool one. The ground should, if possible, be fresh sod-land (preferably pasture) or at most one year removed from the sod. It is unsafe to plant cauliflowers after cauliflowers, or any other plant of the cabbage tribe, though it is sometimes successfully done. Newly cleared land, or land fresh from the sod, is even more desirable for cauliflowers than for cabbages. On new land the crop is not only less subject to disease and the attacks of insects, but its growth is likely to be more satisfactory, even without manure, or with only a moderate amount, than it is on old land, however well manured.

FERTILIZERS.

The cauliflower is a gross feeder, and land intended for this crop can hardly be made too rich. Barn-yard manure is usually employed, and there is nothing better for general use. Commercial fertilizers—potash, soda and phosphates—are also good, especially to promote heading. The wild plant from which the cauliflower is derived being a native of the sea-shore, common salt seems particularly adapted to it. Kelp, or sea-weed, is used with advantage where it can be obtained.

If barn-yard manure is not too coarse, plowing it under in moderate amount will, in addition to its fertilizing effect, help to keep the land moist. Where the cabbage maggot is troublesome the use of fresh stable manure is thought to promote the attack of that insect, and therefore only well rotted manure is recommended. Of course a larger amount of manure may be safely applied if it is well rotted than if it is coarse and strawy. Liquid manure is used by many growers, being applied a few weeks before planting, and from time to time during the season. Water-closet contents, diluted or composted, and applied either in the liquid or powdered form, is one of the best of fertilizers for the cauliflower, but it should not be used too freely, or too late in the season. All coarse or concentrated fertilizers should be applied at least two weeks before the time for transplanting, and such as are applied on the surface should be well mixed with the soil.

SOWING THE SEED.

The preparation of the seed-bed will vary according to circumstances. I formerly grew the plants for the fall crop in beds elevated two or three feet above the ground, in order to escape the flea beetle, but in later years I have grown a portion of the plants in the open ground. This method requires less care, and is now usually practiced by large growers, though it sometimes fails, for the reason stated. Remedies for the flea beetle will be found in another chapter. The soil in which the plants are to be grown should be rich and fine, rather light, and improved, if necessary, with a little of the finest old rotted manure. A small amount of lime or ashes raked into the soil is a benefit, and is thought to prevent the attack of the cabbage maggot, though its value, if any, for this purpose, is slight. An old brush-heap burnt off makes a favorite place for sowing cauliflower and cabbage seed, but it is seldom that market gardeners care to go out of their way to get such a place. The large cauliflower growers of Long Island usually sow the seed in drills across one end of the field in which the crop is to be grown, raking into the soil before sowing, a moderate dressing of some commercial fertilizer.

It is often recommended to sow the seed on the north side of a fence, or in some other partially shaded place. I have never seen any necessity for this, and once spoiled a quantity of plants by growing them in the partial shade of some large trees. At the South, as elsewhere stated, it is sometimes necessary to give the young plants shade during the middle of the day if they are started in the summer months.

The seed should always be sown thinly, not only because it is expensive and none should be wasted, but in order that all may have room to develop into healthy and stocky plants. If the weather is at all dry it is well to lay boards, or some other covering, over the seed-bed until the plants begin to come up. This will insure speedy and uniform germination. If this is done the seed may be sown very shallow; otherwise it should be sown at least half an inch deep (or even deeper if the soil is light) and the soil pressed firm after sowing.

Transplanting the young plants in the seed-bed will render them stocky and vigorous, and should always be practiced with the early crop, but if the seed is sown sufficiently thin it is unnecessary with out-door plants intended for the late crop. Some growers, including Mr. Gregory of Massachusetts, practice sowing the seed in hills in the open ground where the plants are to remain. Several seeds are placed in a hill to insure against loss. This method, however, will seldom be found desirable.

To the above may be added the following excellent directions given by Mr. Francis Brill, 'of Riverhead, Long Island, in his pamphlet on the cauliflower: "Occasionally, by reason of drouth, and frequently by reason of the ravages of insects, great difficulty has been exeprienced in growing plants in spring and early summer, which seldom occurs in the fall—at which time, however, the same precautions may be used. Time was when we could circumvent the flea and louse on young plants by the use of lime, tobacco, ashes, soot, etc., but of late

years they seem to have been so very abundant, and
so materially aided in their work of destruction by the
black grub below and the green grub above ground,
that many complete failures have occurred in en-
deavors to grow plants.   To avoid this I recommend
that the ground intended for plants be plowed or
spaded in the fall, and if stable manure is to be
used, let it be well rotted and turned under at this
time, and again work the soil early in the spring, at
this time turning under a good dressing of potash
salts; keep the ground free from weeds by occasional stirring until the time for sowing the seed,
then lay out a bed six feet wide, and as long as you
please; make the surface smooth, and enclose it with
common boards ten or twelve inches in width set
edgewise perpendicularly, one-half their width
under ground and held in place by stakes driven at
the joints and centres.   Within this frame, beginning at either end, dig and thoroughly pulverize the
soil by means of a spading fork, potato fork, or
similar implement, watching closely for any grub
worms which may not have been eradicated by the
previous workings and which we now propose to
keep out by means of the partially sunken boards.

"Fertilizers may, at this time, be applied and
forked under or raked in, using judgment as to
method and quantity, which must be determined by
the previous condition of the soil and the strength

of the material used, remembering that it is not well
to have any chemicals in too close proximity to the
tender rootlets of the young plants; and while poor
soil is no place in which to grow healthy plants,
yet they should not be over stimulated, but the
ground must be in proper condition to keep up a
vigorous and healthy growth. Let this digging be
done in the latter part of the afternoon when the
sun has spent its force and the soil will not dry out
two quickly; rake the bed as you go, and sow the
seed while the surface soil is fresh and moist, using
a ten-inch board as long as your bed is wide, which
place five or six inches from the end or head of the
frame, crosswise, and with a blunt stick, say three-
fourths of an inch in diameter, draw a mark not
more than one-half an inch deep along each edge of
the board; sow the seed thinly in these marks,
using the thumb and finger to guide it; then turning the board twice, sow two more rows, and so
proceed until you have sown several rows, say 12
to 20, when they must be covered, using the back
of a spade, drawing it with some pressure half way
from each side of the bed. A very important part
of this operation which must not be overlooked *is to
get the seed in and covered while the ground is fresh
and damp;* therefore complete the work in sections. At the distance given the hoe can be used
and the soil stirred between the rows, which is

quite essential to a proper growth of the plants, as well as necessary to keep down the weeds.

"The sowing completed, the bed may be covered with old bags or cloth to retain the moisture, which, however, must be removed upon the first signs of the seed germinating; but what is better still, a shade of muslin can be used, supported by the upper edges of the frame and narrow strips laid across, which can remain until the plants are well above ground, when it should be removed, the plants sprinkled with tobacco dust, air slacked lime, ashes or common plaster, and a covering of mosquito netting be substituted for the muslin, which will admit light, air and sunshine, yet be a partial shade, and will help to protect the plants from insects. This cover may be removed during rain weather, and, if you please, every night to give the plants the benefit of the dew.

"I have decided objections to artificial watering of seed-beds, especially when the seed is first sown or in the early stages of growth of the plants, and this may generally be avoided by following the directions just given; but when circumstances may seem to demand otherwise, let the bed be prepared and in the afternoon thoroughly saturated, and toward evening the seed may be sown and covered as above described, but never water the bed after the seed has been sown until the plants are well up, for this has a tendency to pack the surface and cause it to bake and prevent proper germinating of the seed. After the plants are fairly above ground, light waterings at evening may be given, but must be avoided if possible.

" I have not given these precautions for sowing seed in September for wintering over, for the reason that at that season of the year we are comparatively free from insects and drouths."

WHEN TO SOW.

The time for sowing will depend of course on the locality and variety. At the North, half early varieties, intended for the fall crop, are usually sown and set out about the same time as late cabbage. In Western Michigan, in latitude 43°, I have found that Early Paris sown about May 12, and set out about the 20th of June, begins to head in September, and forms its main crop in October, about the time desired. In the latitude of New York City the time for setting out the main crop is from June 20 to the 1st of August. Plants set as late as the 1st of August are intended to head just before winter, and must be of the earliest varieties. The large late varieties, like Autumn Giant, if used at all, must be started early and set out not later than the first of June, as they require the entire season.

Several kinds are often sown to form a succession, but where one has tested a variety and found it adapted to his needs, it is often quite as well to rely upon it almost entirely, and make two or three sowings for a succession if desired. Even a single sowing, well timed, will generally furnish cuttings through the most favorable part of the season. If the seed is of the best quality, and the plants are of uniform size, and all set at the same time, neither too early nor too late, on soil of uniform character, they will in a good season form most of their heads within a short space of time, sometimes within a week; but generally in a given sowing, a few heads will form very early, then the bulk of the crop will come on during three or four weeks, while the remainder will hang on until late, perhaps until winter. No other crop is so much affected in time of maturity by the character of the season as the cauliflower, and even the most experienced growers sometimes fail in getting them to head at the time desired.

The time for starting the plants for the early crop in the North is in February, and the method is described in full in another chapter. They should be set out, as stated, as soon as heavy freezing is past, say about the middle of April. The most unfavorable time of any, and yet the time when the inexperienced are most likely to set them, is about the middle of May, for early varieties set then usually head in August when it is seldom that heads can be obtained of good quality.

PREPARING THE GROUND.

Land intended for cauliflowers should be plowed deeply, as the cauliflower is a deep feeder and delights in a rich. cool subsoil; in fact, with no other plant of the cabbage family is a deep soil so important. The manure, of whatever kind, should be mainly spread upon the ground and plowed under, a smaller amount, in a finely divided state. being harrowed in upon the surface. The plowing should be done at least a month before the plants are to be set, and the land kept well harrowed or cultivated until that time in order to retain the moisture in the soil, and put it in the best condition for the growth of the plants.

SETTING THE PLANTS.

When the time comes for setting the plants it is a good plan to go over the surface with a planker in order to smooth it off, so the marking can be nicely done. This also packs the ground somewhat, so that the plants can be set more firmly. The land may be then marked out, crosswise first, three feet apart, then lengthwise three feet apart for Dwarf Erfurt and all small growing kinds, and four feet apart for Algiers and other large varieties. These are suitable distances for the late crop in ordinary cases, but where land is cheap, and little manure used, except sod turned under, four by four feet is none too much room for the large varieties. The early crop, on the other hand, which is always heavily manured, is sometimes set with the rows as close as two feet apart, and the plants twenty inches apart in the rows. The small size of the heads resulting from close planting is no actual loss, for small heads, if of good quality, are more popular than large ones, and bring a higher price in proportion to their size. The greatest danger from too close setting of the main crop is that the plants may fail to head at all. It is for this reason that cauliflowers are usually set farther apart than cabbages.

The best time to set the plants is just before or after a rain, but they may be set at any time if the soil has been kept damp by frequent cultivation. In dry, clear weather the planting should be done only toward the close of the day. If it should be necessary to apply water at the time of setting, it should be thoroughly done, not less than a quart being placed in each hole which is to receive a plant. Water should never be applied after the plant is set unless loose earth is afterwards thrown over the place, for the compact surface left after the water has been absorbed dries out more rapidly than before.

The plants to be set should not be too large or they will be liable to button, especially if the conditions are in any way unfavorable for growth. If large plants must be used extra pains should be taken in setting, in order that there may be as little check in their growth as possible. With cauliflowers, as with cabbages, large plants are the easiest to make live, but, for the reason stated, it is less desirable to use them.

Setting the plants in shallow trenches, after the manner of celery, is sometimes practised in garden culture. This places the roots where the soil is cool and moist and enables the plants to be watered to good advantage. This method is mainly used in early spring planting, when, besides its convenience in irrigation, it also serves to protect the plants from cold winds. Planting between ridges, as elsewhere described, serves the same purpose of protection. In either case the surface is gradually brought to a level as the plants are cultivated.

CULTIVATION.

In cultivation everything depends on keeping up a steady, vigorous growth, for if the plants are checked in their growth, they are liable either to form small heads prematurely, or to continue their growth so late as to fail to head at all. Level cultivation is usually practiced, the same as in ordinary field crops. Drawing the earth to the stems, as sometimes recommended and practiced abroad, is unnecessary, though with tall growing varieties it serves a useful purpose in preventing the plants being blown over by the wind. Cultivation should continue until the leaves are so large that they are liable to be broken off, or until the plants are nearly ready to head. The application of a mulch of manure or litter at the time cultivation ceases, is an excellent practice, though seldom resorted to. It is important that deep cultivation should cease at the right time, even if the hoe has to be used afterward. The crop may be seriously injured. or at least delayed, by cultivation after the plants be-gin to head. At this time the ground should be undisturbed so that the roots may occupy the entire soil. Dry weather, and the compact nature of the soil after cultivation ceases, check the growth of the plants, and promote the formation of heads, pro-viding the plants have attained a proper age and size. The influence of a firm soil in promoting heading is also seen in the success with which cauli-flowers can frequently be grown after peas or other early crops. In autumn the first sharp frosts ap-pear to be particularly efficacious in starting the plants to heading.

IRRIGATION.

After heading has commenced is the time when irrigation is most needed. An abundance of water at this time will add greatly, both to the quantity and quality of the product, particularly if some fertilizer is added at the same time. Irrigation is not often practiced in this country, except in the arid districts of the West, and occasionally, with the early crop, near a few of our large cities. In Europe, where labor is cheap, it is often resorted to, even where the water has to be carried by hand. Early in the season, if irrigation is needed, once a week is frequent enough to apply the water, but while the plants are heading it may be applied with advantage every day if the weather is dry.

BLANCHING THE HEADS.

The value of cauliflowers for use or market depends almost entirely on their being white and tender. To have them remain in this condition until fully matured, they must be protected from the sun. Heads which are left exposed become yellow in color, or even brownish purple if the sun is very hot. Such heads also acquire a strong, disagreeable flavor.

There are various ways of covering the heads, but it is nearly always done with the leaves of the plant. Early in the season, when the weather is dry and warm, the work may be done during the heat of the day by lapping the leaves, one after another, over the head until it is sufficiently covered, tucking the last leaf under to hold all in place.

Or the leaves may be fastened with a butcher's skewer, or any sharp stick. In Florida, orange thorns are employed for this purpose. Care must be taken not to confine the heads too closely, or they will grow out of shape, besides being liable to heat and become spotted. Later in the season, when the weather is cool and damp, the leaves will be too stiff to be bent down, and the head must then be protected either by placing over it leaves broken from the outer part of the plant, or from stumps from which the heads have already been cut, or by tying the leaves together above the head. The latter is the usual method. rye straw or bast matting being generally used for the purpose. Merely breaking down the inner leaves upon the head is unsatisfactory, as the growth. both of the leaves and the head. soon causes the head to become exposed.

The artificial blanching of the head is most important early in the season, while the sun is hot, and the field should then be gone over as often as every other day for this purpose, taking two rows at a time. Later in the season, during damp, cloudy weather, heads will sometimes reach full size and still be of good color though entirely exposed. It is unsafe to leave them in this way, however, as a little change in color seriously affects their market value. Covering the heads appears also to cause them to grow larger and remain solid longer than they otherwise would, particularly early in the season.

PROTECTING FROM FROST.

Another object, late in the season, in covering the heads, is to protect them from frost. A frosted cauliflower is practically worthless for market, as it is nearly certain to turn black on the surface after one or two days' exposure. Freezing, in fact, is one of the most frequent sources of loss on cauliflowers late in the season, and as this is the most favorable time of the year for them to head, it is necessary to take particular care to guard against loss from this cause. We frequently have a few hard frosts early in October, which spoil such heads as are nearly mature, unless they have been protected. After this there may be a month or more of good weather, during which the bulk of the crop may come to maturity. The heads are protected from frost in the same manner as from the sun, but it is best not to have the leaves lie directly on the head. Protection is particularly needed as the heads approach maturity, as they are then more easily injured than while small. Heads which are well covered will usually stand eight or ten degrees of frost without injury, depending on the amount of cloudiness and moisture present. In cool, moist, cloudy weather, frosted heads will sometimes recover and show no injury. It is even possible for heads to become frozen solid and come out in good condition, but this rarely occurs, and requires that the thawing take place in the most favorable manner possible. Cutting the frozen heads with their leaves, throwing them in shallow heaps upon the ground, and covering with straw, will sometimes bring them out in good condition: also throwing them into water but little above the freezing point. The safest way, however, if possible, is to cook the heads at once, putting the frozen heads directly into boiling water. Treated in this manner they exhibit little or no effect of the freezing.

The safest way, in case heavy freezing is apprehended, is to cut and remove to a place of safety all heads which have attained half their size or more.

CUTTING THE HEADS.

The frequency of cutting will depend on the season of the year. In summer, the heads will remain at the proper stage for cutting no more than a day or two, while late in autumn they may often be left a week before becoming overgrown.

Frequent cutting is at all times desirable, however, as it is best to let the heads get as large as they will before becoming loose and warty. The gain in size not only increases their selling price, but the flavor also appears to improve as the heads approach maturity. Immature heads, though mild and tender, have less flavor than those which are full grown. It is better, however, to cut a head too soon than to leave it too long, for a small solid head will sell for more than a large loose one. To judge when a head has reached full size requires some experience. The size of course, will depend on that of the plant, but its size in proportion to that of the plant is perhaps the most common point by which one judges when it is ready to cut. The head, when it approaches maturity, rises within the leaves and bulges the latter outward, so that one can often tell at some distance which heads are about ready. The surface of the head, as it approaches maturity looses its polished appearance and becomes more distinctly grained. This change, if it does not go too far, does not detract from its appearance and value. To examine a head, do not untie the top, but part the leaves at the side. If there are signs of cracking or breaking it is ready to cut. The heads should be cut with about an inch of stalk and two or three full circles of leaves. A long thin-bladed knife is best to cut with.

The best time of the day in which to cut the heads, if for home use, or a near market, is in the morning while the dew is on, as they will then remain longer in a fresh state than if cut latter in the day. If to pack for a distant market, the heads will carry and keep better if cut when dry, but on a cool day or towards evening.

HANDLING.

The heads must be handled with care to prevent the "flower" becoming bruised or soiled in any way. A bruise will turn black in a short time, the same as a frosted surface, and thus injure the sale . of the head. The heads can be handled most safely if the leaves are left on, and these had best be left entire until the plants are taken to the pack-ing shed; and for a near market they may even be left on to advantage until the plants are ready to be exposed for sale. The main object of their removal is in order that the heads may be readily inspected.

TRIMMING.

This is often done in the field, but, as just stated, it had better be delayed until the heads are carried to the place for packing. To trim them, take hold of a head near the butt with one hand, holding it upright against you, then with a turning motion, cut clear around the head, leaving the cut ends of the leaves projecting about an inch above the edge of the head. This exposes as much of the head as can be seen at one view, and the leaves as left pro-tect the margin from bruises. The butt should be cut off smooth, and there should be left about two layers of leaves

The heads at the time of packing should be free from moisture, and if the leaves are a trifle wilted they will pack all the better. Flour barrels, or barrels of that size, are best to pack in, as cauliflowers are now usually sold at wholesale by the barrel. Barrel-crates of the same size are also coming into use, especially for the early crop, as the heads are liable to heat in hot weather if packed in close barrels. Each cauliflower at the time of packing is now usually wrapped in strong soft white paper, the edges of the paper being tucked between the leaves and head. The heads are then placed in the barrels, commencing at the outside, laying them upon their sides facing in, and filling the center with smaller heads. Continue each layer in this way until the barrel is a little more than full. Pack as solid as possible. Cover with canvass or bagging, putting it under the top hoop and pressing it down by driving down and nailing the hoop. Tea-chest matting, which usually costs nothing, may be used for covers if desired.

It may be added that cauliflowers are sometimes packed in their own leaves, just as they come from the field, or all the leaves may be removed but one or two which are to be folded over the head. It usually pays, however, to use paper, but this must be white, or else when bruised it will stain the heads.

Sometimes, when the cauliflowers are to be sold at retail, sugar-barrels are used to pack in, as they cost less than other barrels and are larger. They are always clean and sweet, and do not make too large a package, as cauliflowers are not heavy.

Small slatted crates are also a favorite package in which to ship cauliflowers, particularly early in the season. Large crates, such as are sometimes used for cabbages, are entirely unsuitable.

A method of packing cauliflowers for shipment employed in Denmark, is described as follows: "The heads are to be cut off in a dry state, but not wilted, and with only an inch of stalk. The leaves are to be removed, with the exception of a couple of the inner courses, which should be cut down to such a length as to meet when they are bent gently together over the head. Pack in clean, open neat-looking crates or boxes, in the bottom of which put a few leaves, and on these the cauliflower heads, which should be of a uniform size for each crate. Pack closely and firmly in layers, taking care, however, not to bruise the tender heads. All the heads in a layer should turn in the same direction, being laid sidewise, and the next layer in the opposite direction, respectively, with top and stem. On the top of the heads fill in with leaves until the cover will press the whole contents so tight as to prevent the heads from moving during transportation."

The price of cauliflowers is less subject to fluct-
uation than that of most other vegetables. There
is comparatively little competition between different
localities, and about the only causes of low prices
are temporary and local over-production, and forced
sales caused by damaged stock. One year with
another, a dollar and a half a dozen may be realized
on good heads, which is more than double the average price of cabbages. Contracts are taken, however, at as low as fifty cents a dozen to supply pickle-
factories. Under favorable conditions fully as large
a percentage of cauliflowers will head as of cabbages,
so that in a good location, with proper care, the cauliflower crop is a profitable one. It may be well to
remind growers, however, that one should not attempt
to sell a large quantity of cauliflowers in a small
market, for even at a low price people will not buy
largely of what they are not accustomed to using.
But it is surprising to what an extent a market may
be developed for this vegetable. No one who has
once used the cauliflower will thereafter do without
it, if it can be obtained at a reasonable price. There
is absolutely no necessary limit to the market for
this vegetable, providing reasonable care is exercised
in creating and supplying the demand. The price
in this country ought always to be maintained if possible at at least double that of cabbages, not only on
account of the greater delicacy of the cauliflower,

but because of the greater care needed in its production, and the uncertainty of the crop, owing to unfavorable seasons and other causes. I could easily quote examples of extraordinary profits made in growing the cauliflower, as well as instances of repeated failure. Cases of both kinds of experience are given elsewhere in the present volume. I have here only attempted to show what may be reasonably expected.

KEEPING.

More attention is being paid of late years to the keeping of cauliflowers in winter, and it is now customary with some to plant a small late crop for the purpose of winter heading. Most growers, however, will have more or less unheaded plants at the end of nearly every season which can be used for this purpose.

William Falconer, of Long Island, sows Extra Early Erfurt about July 1, pots the young plants, and sets them in the open field after early potatoes have come off. In November the plants that show signs of heading are stripped of the larger outer leaves, then taken up and set close together in beds and covered with hot-bed sash. In cold weather straw or thatch is added. In this way the plants continue to give heads until February. Plants which have begun to head may be taken up in the same way and set in a cellar. Just enough moisture should be given to keep them from wilting, as, if too much is given, they are liable to rot. Fully headed cauliflowers are difficult to keep. If hung up in a cellar in the way cabbages are frequently kept, they wilt and become strong in flavor and dark in color. This may be remedied with a few heads by cutting off the stem a few inches below the head before they are hung up, hollowing out the stem and filling the hollow with water. It is said that the heads will keep in good condition for a long time if packed in slightly damp muck. A simple way of preserving partly headed plants out of doors is to take them up with as much earth as possible and set them close together in trenches, after the manner of celery, placing boards at the sides, and in cold weather a covering of straw overhead. In this way the heads are easily accessible and keep in good condition.

A method employed in Scotland for preserving cauliflower is to bury them in a dry place, heads downward and roots exposed, in the ordinary manner of burying cabbages. They are said to keep well by this method from November to January. The leaves are folded over the heads to keep them from coming in contact with the soil.

Another method, employed in Denmark, is to make a bed of moist sand about four inches deep in a cool room protected against frost; the floor

had better be of asphalt, cement or the like.
Toward the end of autumn the heads are cut with
a piece of the stem three or four inches in length,
which is stuck into the sand. All the leaves are
removed except the inner course, which must be
cut down pretty closely, and the heads then covered
with flower pots.

Still another method, employed where hard
freezlng is not anticipated, is to take up the plants
and set them out in a slanting position close
together out of doors with the heads to the north, as
is done with cabbages.

Pulling up the plants and throwing them on
their sides will protect the heads from a moderate
degree of cold, and can be resorted to upon the
sudden approach of cold weather. Cutting the
heads with plenty of leaves and throwing them in
long low heaps, faces downward, will preserve
them in the cool, damp weather of early winter for
a considerable time, and the heads, even in this
condition, will increase somewhat in size.

It will sometimes happen, early in the season,
that one desires to retard the development of the
head until a convenient time for marketing. For
this purpose the plants may be lifted, when the
heads are nearly mature, and set under a shed or
elsewhere in the shade.

It may be well here to remind those who grow

only a few plants in a garden, and who wish to
prolong the season, that several cuttings may be
taken from a single head if desired. A portion of
the head should be left each time. Occasionally,
but not often, a stump will sprout and form a second crop. A method of accelerating the formation
of heads, which is practiced in Ireland, may also be
worth recording. It consists in slitting the stalk
from near the ground upward toward the heart,
and placing a stick in the slit to prevent the parts
reuniting. The soil is then drawn up around the
cut, and the plant staked to prevent its breaking
off. It is said that plants so treated will form their
heads from six to eight days earlier than they
otherwise would.

CHAPTER IV.

THE EARLY CROP.

I cannot do better in treating of this crop than to first quote the following, by the late Peter Henderson, of New York City, from his work on "Gardening for Pleasure":

"There is quite an ambition among amateur gardeners to raise early cauliflower, but as the conditions necessary to success with this are not quite so easy to command as with most other vegetables, probably not one in three who try it succeed. In England, and most places on the Continent of Europe, it is the most valued of all vegetables, and is grown there nearly as easily as early cabbages. But it must be remembered that the temperature there is on the average ten degrees lower at the time it matures (June) than with us; besides, their atmosphere is much more humid, two conditions essential to its proper development. I will briefly state how early cauliflowers can be most successfully grown here. First, the soil must be well broken, and pulverized by spading to at least a foot in depth, mixing through it a layer of three or four inches of strong well-rotted stable manure. The plants may be either those from seed sown last fall

and wintered over in cold frames, or else started
from seeds sown in January or February in a hot-
bed or greenhouse, and planted in small pots or
boxes, so as to make plants strong enough to be set
out as soon as the soil is fit to work, which, in this
latitude, is usually the first week in April. We are
often applied to for cauliflower plants as late as
May, but the chances of their forming heads when
planted in May are slim indeed. The surest way
to secure the heading of cauliflowers is to use what
are called hand-glasses. These are usually made
about two feet square, which gives room enough
for three or four plants of cauliflower until they are
so far forwarded that the glass can be taken off.
When the hand-glass is used the cauliflowers may
be planted out in any warm border early in March
and covered by them. This covering protects them
from frost at night, and gives the necessary increase
of temperature for growth during the cold weeks
of March and April; so that by the first week in
May, if the cauliflower has been properly hardened
off by ventilating (by tilting up the hand-glasses
on one side) they may be taken off altogether and
then used to forward tomatoes, melons or cucumbers. If the weather is dry the cauliflowers will
be much benefitted by being thoroughly soaked
with water twice or thrice a week.   *   *   *
The two best varieties of cauliflower we have

found as yet [1875] are the Dwarf Erfurt and Early Paris."

Notwithstanding the care required for the early crop, the same writer states in his earlier work on "Gardening for Profit," (published in 1867, during a period of high prices,) that "for the past four or five years cauliflowers [early] have been one of my most profitable crops. I have, during that time, grown about one acre each year, which has certainly averaged $1,500. On one occasion the crop proved almost an entire failure, owing to unusual drought in May; while, on another occasion, with an unusually favorable season, it sold at nearly $3,000 per acre. The average price for all planted is about $15 per 100, and as from 10,000 to 12,000 are grown to the acre, it will result in nearly the average before named—$1,500 per acre. Unlike cabbages, however, only a limited number is yet sold, and I have found that an acre of them has been quite as much as could be profitably grown in one garden."

The above, by the late well-known New York seedsman and market-gardener, though written nearly forty years ago, is true to-day, so far as the general profitableness of the cauliflower is concerned, and the extra care required with the early crop.

The chief condition of success with early cauliflowers is that they shall head before hot weather comes on. To this end the earliest varieties are chosen, and they are set as early as possible in the spring, and pushed rapidly forward, as stated, by using protection if necessary, and by high manuring. It is an advantage to set the early plants between ridges, as is done with early cabbage. The ridges hold the sun and keep off the cold winds, and the furrows between carry off the surface water. The plants are best set upon the south or east side of the ridges, near the base. A good furrow with an ordinary plow forms a sufficient ridge.

Formerly it was thought necessary to start the plants in the fall, but since the newer early sorts have been produced, this is being abandoned. Fall sowing has never been as successful in the Northern United States as in England, and the failures to grow cauliflowers successfully in this country have often resulted from adhering to the methods employed in the Old World. Plants started in hot-beds in February, and properly hardened off, receive but little check when set out, and make a better growth than those which have been wintered over.

In the latitude of Virginia and Maryland, wintering over the young plants may be resorted to, and for gardeners in that latitude the methods adopted in England will be well worth studying, even if they can not be literally followed. The time for sowing the seed should be so gauged that the plants shall be neither too large nor too small during the coldest months. If too small they will not be sufficiently hardy to winter over; if too large they will be likely to button instead of forming fully developed heads.

When the young plants are transplanted into their winter quarters they should be set deeply, as the stem is the part most easily injured by cold; the same rule of planting deeply should be followed in the first plantings in the open ground in spring.

Wintering in the open air in a warm sheltered situation is preferable, where it can be done, to wintering under frames, for plants so exposed will be most healthy and will continue their growth with least interruption in the spring.

Plants wintered under glass require considerable room, and as much air as can be safely given. If pots are used, care must be taken not to have them too small, or to allow them to become entirely filled with the roots, for this will have a tendency to cause the plants to button.

BUTTONING.

I cannot perhaps do better than to mention here such other causes as have this same tendency. Anything which checks the growth of the plants when they are a few inches high is liable to pro-

4

duce this result—such as leaving them too long in the seed-bed, withholding water, poor soil, too much crowding. After the plants are set out, a cold rainy time or badly drained land may have the same effect; also a very hot time, if the soil is dry and the plants are not growing well. The check occasioned by the transplanting may also cause the plants to button, if they have become large, and the soil or weather is unfavorable. On this account it is unsafe to let cauliflower plants get as large as cabbage plants sometimes are when transplanted.

I will close this topic by quoting two paragraphs from *The Garden*, an English journal from which I have already taken much valuable information. The first is by a person who signs himself "D. T. F.," who says:

"Cambrian [a previous writer] attributes this to over-manuring, and no doubt this frequently causes buttoning, but over-frosting is quite as injurious as over-manuring; and the hard frost which we had here on the 1st of April seems to be sending all the exposed plants into buttons, whilst those protected only with glass lights seem safe and sound and are spreading their leaves wide and looking extremely promising."

The next writer, Mr. Gilbert, adds:

"The whole of my Early London cauliflowers

have buttoned, but not the Walcheren, at least at present. I hear, too, this is the case in many parts of the country. I have for years noted that after a cold severe winter and a warm spring both cauliflowers and cabbages 'bolt,' but this season having been quite the reverse I thought they might have escaped."

Another writer calls attention to the fact that plants which have been nursed or protected too much during winter are more apt to button when set out in the spring than those which have been more exposed.

CHAPTER V.

CAULIFLOWER REGIONS OF THE UNITED STATES.

A comparatively small portion of the United States is well adapted to the growth of cauliflower. The climate for the most part is too dry. The districts suited to its cultivation are often of very limited area, and are determined by local causes affecting the distribution of moisture and the character of the soil. The manner of treating the crop, and the degree of care necessary for successful results, will therefore depend largely on the locality where it is grown. For the purpose of giving more definite information on these points, the country may be divided into the following cauliflower regions:

THE UPPER ATLANTIC COAST.

This includes the greatest number of localities where cauliflower culture has thus far been successfully conducted in the United States. The region is comparatively well watered, and contains a great diversity of soil and situation. More good markets are found here than elsewhere. The heart of this cauliflower region is now found upon the north shore of Long Island, where there is a strong soil, in a damp climate, within easy reach of the New York and other large markets. Two crops are grown here, the spring and fall. Wm. Falconer, of Queen's County, states that for the early crop he sows the seed in a hot-house in February, and gradually gives the plants more room and cooler quarters until they are ready for the open ground. The varieties he uses are Henderson's Snowball, Early Erfurt, Stadtholder and Lenormand. He has repeatedly attempted to grow the spring crop from fall-sown plants, but they have almost invariably buttoned, however late the seed was sown, or however slightly the plants were protected. Occasionally, also, the February-sown plants of Henderson's Snowball and Erfurt will button.

For the main fall crop the same four varieties above mentioned are sown out of doors about May 18th, at the time of sowing late cabbage. For a later crop he makes another sowing a month later. These last usually begin to head about the last of November and are taken up and protected to furnish a supply during the winter. Mr. C. E. Swezey, of Suffolk County, says that more money is undoubtedly made to the acre on cauliflower than any other crop. He finds the early crop the most profitable, although the most expensive. For this crop he uses seventy-five tons of the best horse manure per

acre, and for the late crop about half that amount.
The variety he prefers is Henderson's Snowball,
this with the Early Erfurt being the only kinds he
uses.

Francis Brill, in his book on "Farm Gardening
and Seed Growing," said, in 1872, "For the past two
years the farmers of the east end of Long Island,
especially about the village of Mattituck, have
planted largely of cauliflower, being incited by the
successful experiments of some who have removed
here from the west end, who were formerly engaged
in growing vegetables for the New York markets.
The past season the crop has succeeded admirably,
and large profits have been realized by growers in
this vicinity, and this by men, many of whom are
inexperienced in the cultivation of this or any other
vegetable for market; and, moreover, the most of it
was grown at the worst possible season of the year.
As a general rule, cauliflowers do not succeed well
on old land, and much of the land hereabouts is new,
and but little of it indeed has ever been used for
cabbages or anything of this nature.   But beyond
a doubt it is the humid saline atmosphere of this
section which makes the cultivation of this vegetable a success.   Protracted drouths are here almost
unknown, and even during the temporary absence
of rain in the summer months the air does not seem
so dry and withering, so to speak, as in sections

more remote from the ocean, the Sound and the great salt water bays by which we are surrounded." The varieties he mentions are Early Erfurt and Early Paris for the first crop, the Nonpareil and [or] Half Early Paris for a succession, with Lenormand and Walcheren for late.

The same author, in his work entitled "Cauliflowers and How to Grow Them," published in 1886, says: "The cultivation of cauliflower in the eastern towns of Suffolk County, N. Y., familiarly known as the east end of Long Island, was begun at Mattituck about sixteen years ago, upon a small scale, as an experiment, by one or two gardeners from the west end who were formerly engaged in growing vegetables for New York markets. The success which attended these experiments, and the subsequent efforts of some of our farmers, who by reason of reported great profits, were induced to take up the cultivation of this crop, has been an incentive to others, until at the present time an East End farm without an acre or more of cauliflower is an exception, while in the towns of Riverhead and Southold many farmers grow from five to fifteen acres each, and in the other towns of Suffolk County the business is largely on the increase. As a rule the crop has done well, subject of course to the ravages of insects, drouths, etc., which have at times been serious drawbacks; especially was this the case in 1884, when the crop was almost a total failure, but never before had we experienced such a protracted drouth or such an abundance of insects of every known species, and only those who were in advance of the drouth, or who had sown seed very late, succeeded in getting heads for market, but the few who were thus situated received almost fabulous prices for their product." The following year he says the crop was remarkably successful, more than 100,000 barrels being shipped from Suffolk county to the New York markets during the months of October and November. "Prices this year have ranged from ten dollars early in the season down to one dollar and twenty-five cents a barrel during the glut, when large quantities were sold to picklers at one cent per pound for clean trimmed clear curd or flower. As a rule early and very late cauliflowers bring the best prices. * * * * * Experience has taught us that stable manure applied at the time of planting, except for the earliest spring crop, is often injurious, and I advise applying stable manure plentifully to the crop of the preceding year, or otherwise let it be turned under at the fall plowing, or if well rotted at the first spring plowing, and at the time of planting apply commercial fertilizers, or, as they are sometimes called, patent manures, using whatever brand you may have the most confidence in. The competition between manufacturers has become so great that all are compelled to be at least partially honest, and several prepare a special fertilizer for cauliflower and cabbage which works admirably. Our best growers all use German potash salts, or Kainit, about 13 per cent. actual potash, one ton to the acre; or sulphate of potash, equal to 27 per cent. actual potash; or muriate of potash, equal, to 45 per cent. actual potash, about one half a ton to the acre. The relative cost per ton, of these is $16.00 for Kainit, $38.00 for sulphate and $45.00 for muriate—these are present prices, but the market is subject to fluctuations. These should be evenly applied broadcast and turned under at the spring plowing, and from one half a ton to one ton of fertilizer to the acre should be applied in the same manner on the surface, and harrowed in at the last preparation of the soil. Of late many have been using fish guano. which is the scrap or flesh and bone refuse from the Menhaden oil-rendering establishments, in connection with potash salts, with excellent results; in fact Captain Edward Hawkins, of Jamesport, one of our most successful growers, uses nothing else, applying one ton of each to the acre. Very good cauliflowers have been grown by opening furrows, placing the fertilizer therein, and covering so as to form ridges; but I advise broadcast manuring and flat cultivation for this crop, as I am fully convinced that one acre in proper shape and condition will pay much better than two acres only half fertilized. Pure, fine ground bone, one ton to the acre, plowed under will be found beneficial, especially so in carrying the plants out at the time of heading, but it is scarcely stimulating enough for the early requirements of the plants. Well rotted stable manure may be used to advantage, freshly applied and plowed under, for early spring planting of cold-frame or hot-bed plants which are expected to mature before extremely hot-dry weather, but it has no special advantage except to warm up the soil. * * * The great crop with us is during the months of October and November, for which seed is sown from May 15 to June 25, and the plants set from the middle of June to the last of August according to the kind." The varieties named for spring planting are, "Erfurt Extra Dwarf Earliest," and "Small Leaved Erfurt," both being also good for the fall crop, the latter for this crop being sown as late as July 1st. The Algiers, a standard sort for fall, is sown from May 15 to June 1. Mr. Brill adds: "Every known sort has been tested by our growers, and I have had in one field eighty six samples, comprising every known variety and sub-variety often repeated, grown from seed procured from every possible source, and with the exception of one or two sorts, which have done well under peculiarly favorable conditions and circumstances, all have been positively condemned except those above named." The varieties referred to are the Dwarf Erfurt strains (including Henderson's), the Algiers, and the Early and Half Early Paris—the latter two being now superceded by the former.

C. H. Allen, in the *American Agriculturist* for 1889, page 297, says: " No section of the United States seems so well adapted to the growing of the cauliflower as the northeastern part of Long Island, N. Y. For the earliest crop a piece of heavy sod ground is plowed during the month of April. It is then spread with fish scrap at the rate of one ton to the acre, which is thoroughly harrowed in. A strip is then prepared for sowing seed, by raking the ground until it is in good condition; the first sowing of seed is made May 15. The seed for the main crop is sown ten to twenty days later. When the plants are ready to set the ground is again plowed in an opposite direction from the first plowing and then spread with muriate of potash at the rate of half a ton to the acre, or if fish scrap cannot be procured, some standard fertilizer is used after the second plowing without the addition of muriate of potash. The Early Dwarf Erfurt and Snowball are the most popular varieties. The Algiers has been largely used, but for the past two or three seasons has done very poorly, and will not be grown in the future. The plants are set three feet apart each way. This applies to Erfurt and Snowball; Algiers requires the rows four feet apart."

The *American Garden* for 1889, page 59, says: "Almost nine-tenths of all the cauliflowers that come to the New York market are grown in Suffolk County on Long Island, and this industry is said to bring about $200,000 a year to the county. Success with cauliflower culture has been very indifferent in other parts of Long Island and elsewhere where tried."

A New Jersey market-gardener described his experience as follows a few years ago in the New York *Tribune*: "Among the many uncertain crops, the cauliflower stands prominent, for very often under the best culture, it fails to produce a head on an acre, although the usual outlay for preparing and manuring the ground preparatory to planting will be at least twice as much as for a crop of late cabbage. But when a full crop of cauliflower is raised, the profits will average three times that of the cabbage in the same market. This being the case, it is not strange that every means known to the profession should be resorted to with the hope of getting year after year maximum crops of this vegetable. But, as yet, no plan has been discovered, under our burning July and August sun, that will make cauliflower head with certainty every season.

Any practical man, with strong ground well manured, can every now and then raise a crop of cauliflower. But this partial success one year does very
often prove a decided loss in the long run, for the
reason that it often happens three times the amount
realized from this crop will be spent in the attempt
to raise another just like it, with the determination
not to give up. This has been my experience,
although the experiments are made now on a much
smaller scale than formerly. Last year I set out
2,500 plants, and only marketed 500 from the patch;
the failure was owing to late planting. To avoid
any such mistake this year, the ground was made
ready for planting early in July, and by the middle
of the month some 1,800 plants set out. The
ground in this case was richer and more mellow at
the time of planting than last year, and the cultivation was about the same. At first these plants
grew vigorously, but late in August they were
checked from some unknown cause, and from this
check they did not recover. Some of the lower leaves
had turned yellow and dropped off, leaving the
stalks almost bare, while others have made no new
growth since. Judging from present appearances,
there will not be twenty-five sizeable heads out of
the 1,800 planted. This is rather discouraging,
but one has to take the good with the bad in farming or gardening. Too late to remedy the error it

was found that the variety planted was Walcheren instead of the Erfurt, a variety that has given me more profitable returns for the last six years than any other, unless it may be the Half Early Paris."

In New England the crop is more uncertain than on Long Island. W. H. Bull, of Hampden County, Massachusetts, finds the crop profitable about one year in three. Formerly, he says, when cauliflowers were a new thing, any kind of a head would sell, but now only the best will bring a paying price. The loose, leafy, purple, or otherwise discolored heads produced in hot, dry weather, are hardly worth hauling to market. He finds the Extra Early Erfurt about as good as Henderson's Snowball. He sows the seed in April for a fall crop. If sown after the first week in May the plants fail to head before frost.

Around Boston the cauliflower is grown quite successfully, and, as elsewhere stated, seed is occasionally produced there. The variety formerly grown for the main crop was an improved form of Early Paris, called Boston Market, but this is now displaced by the new Extra Early Erfurt strains. It may be mentioned here that around Montreal the fall crop is very successfully grown.

THE LAKE REGION.

In the region of the Great Lakes there are many localities having a suitable soil in which cauliflower may be grown to good advantage. The moist atmosphere, which renders much of this region so well adapted to the cultivation of fruit, favors the growth of the cauliflower. In this region the fall crop is the one mainly grown, and the half-early varities, such as Early Paris and Early London have been chiefly used, though the earlier Erfurt varities are now largely grown.

Detroit, Grand Rapids, and other Michigan cities are comparatively well supplied with home-grown cauliflower.

In Western Michigan there is considerable high, rolling land, of a deep loamy character. covered originally with a heavy growth of hard-wood timber. It was on such land as this, in Ottawa County, that the writer grew cauliflower very successfully between the years 1870 and 1884. The land had but recently been cleared of its timber, and it seldom received any other fertilizer than the heavy June-grass sod which was turned under. The method of preparing the ground was the same as for any other farm crop, and the plants, mainly of the Early Paris variety, were set out about the last of June, usually four feet apart each way. They were given good care, and generally began to head in September, at the time of the autumnal equinox, when there is usually a week or two of cool, rainy weather. Following this, early in October, there are generally a few hard frosts which injure some of the heads if they are not kept well covered and closely cut. The main cauliflower season then comes on, running through October and the first half of November. In a warm, late season nearly all the plants will have headed, and the heads have been sold before cold weather, but when winter comes on early, a portion of the plants will be still undeveloped; these are either gathered and stored, as elsewhere described, or used for feeding stock. My crop was marketed at Grand Rapids and Chicago, and was considered the finest sent to either of those cities. Its excellence was attributed mainly to the deep new fertile soil, which never suffered from drouth under proper cultivation, and to the moist climate, due to the surrounding forests and the proximity to Lake Michigan.

At South Haven, on the immediate shore of Lake Michigan, the upland is mainly too heavy for the best growth of cauliflower. Mr. Sheffer says: (Mich. Ag. Rep. 1888, p. 287) " We have the advantage of cheap lands, cheap transportation to a boundless market, and a moist climate, all making celery and cauliflower desirable crops. For cauliflower, the proper soil is the first essential. If planted on uplands it will fail nine times out of ten, unless set so late as to head up just before winter. But it is better to grow it on low wet soils that can be ditched

5

and the crop headed earlier. It can be marketed as far away as Philadelphia."

In Kent County, with which I am familiar, the cauliflower is successfully cultivated by many gardeners, but, as the air is drier, more care is required there in selecting the soil, the crop being usually grown on bottom lands favorably situated with regard to moisture, and containing an abundance of vegetable matter. It is occasionally grown on muck, but such land is not as reliable as that of a heavier character. On the light, sandy, and gravelly uplands, which abound in this county, the cultivation of the cauliflower is seldom attempted, and always fails, except in unusually wet seasons, although when such land is heavily manured, the cabbage may be grown successfully.

At Duluth, Minnesota, near the western end of Lake Superior, I have seen as fine cauliflowers growing as I ever saw anywhere. The soil was black loamy, upland.

Mr. J. S. Brocklehurst, of Oneota, in the same county, considers his locality unsurpassed for the cauliflower.

In Northern Wisconsin there is considerable territory which is excellent for cauliflower. In 1890, the first, second and third prizes offered by James Vick, for the best heads of Vick's Ideal were all awarded to growers in Eau Clare County, Wisconsin.

The recent introduction of very early varities is likely to have an important result in extending the cultivation of the cauliflower, in the extreme Northern States and Canada, where the soil and climate are in many places peculiarly adapted to it, but where the seasons are so short that it has not heretofore been successfully grown.

Around Chicago much of the soil is unsurpassed for this vegetable, and large quantities of it are grown, but not enough to supply its local demand.

The most successful cultivators of this vegetable near Chicago are the market gardeners in the Holland settlement south of the city, and the Germans on the north. All are more successful with the late crop than with the early. One of the most successful of these growers sometimes sets his plants as late as the first of August, using seed direct from friends in Holland.

In Mahoning County, Ohio, which may be included, for convenience, in the Lake Region, Mr. Milton, who makes a specialty of the cauliflower, states that it is a good paying crop, but requires high cultivation, and if possible a moist soil. He states that he has tried all the varieties in cultivation, and finds a great difference in seed of the same variety from different growers. For the early crop he one year planted Henderson's Snowball, extra selected Early Erfurt, and Vick's Ideal, and found, owing to a drouth which set in just as the heads began to form, that the last variety was the only one which gave paying heads. For a late crop he generally uses Half-Early Paris, but has had good success with Algiers in a warm season. This variety must be started very early, however, in order to head before winter.

THE PRAIRIE REGION.

Prairie soil is usually well adapted to the cauliflower, and in favorable seasons a good crop is obtained, but such seasons are so little to be depended on in this region that cauliflower culture on a large scale is only profitable here under irrigation, or in restricted localities where the soil is naturally moist.

The gardeners around St. Louis have good success in growing cauliflower on the bottom land. Professor L. R. Taft says, "During two of the years I lived in Missouri it was very hot and dry and on the heavy clay soil of most of the state cauliflower, as a field crop, was a failure. I had good success, however, by planting one foot apart in cold frames from which lettuce had been taken; they were watered as required and during the hottest weather were protected to some extent by means of lath screens."

One disadvantage in this uncertainty of a crop in the West is its effect upon the market. A product which is rarely seen in the market brings a low price when abundant and fails to bring a high price in times of scarcity. Few people use it, and these do not become so accustomed to it as to be willing to pay a high price for it when it is scarce.

Mr. Riche, of Iowa, tells in a report of the Iowa Horticultural Society, how, in 1884, he overstocked the Dubuque market with 8000 heads. A Mr. Smith relates how, a few years previous, he was obliged to sell 4000 heads for a little over one cent per head; yet in this same market more familiar products often bring high prices. Another Iowa gardener grew a field of cauliflower by mistake, having purchased the seed for cabbage, and found himself unable to sell the crop at all!

In the irrigated districts of the West, cauliflower is grown to great perfection. One of the largest cauliflowers on record, four feet three inches in circumference, was grown in Colorado under irrigation in 1881. A moist atmosphere is less important than plenty of water at the root, especially at the time of heading, when it should be supplied, if possible, in small amount every day. The somewhat saline character of the soil in the dry regions also favors the growth of this crop whenever a sufficient supply of water is given.

At the Colorado experiment station sixteen varieties were grown under irrigation in 1888 (see table under Variety Tests), of which Henderson's Snowball and Extra Early Erfurt gave the best results. At the Arkansas station, the following year, out of twelve varieties these two were the only ones that produced heads. At the South Dakota station, Henderson's Snowball and Haskell's Favorite, a variety apparently identical with it, gave good results.

CAULIFLOWER IN THE SOUTH.

The cauliflower, as a market crop, is but little grown in the South, but there is no good reason why it should not become extensively cultivated there. The chief hindrances to its cultivation in the South have been the lack of high priced local markets, and the liability of the heads to heat during transportation to the North.

The most favorable localities for growing this vegetable in the South are near the Gulf and Atlantic coasts, especially near the mouths of rivers where there is an alluvial soil and a moist atmosphere. The cauliflower is better adapted than the cabbage to a warm climate, but heavier soil is required for it in the South than at the North.

W. F. Massey, of the North Carolina experiment station, says that fall-sown plants are the only ones worth growing in that latitude. The seed should be sown in September. The crop should head not later than March or April, as the heat is too great after April for good heads. By forcing, the plants may be headed in the frames in winter. More heat and protection are needed for this than in merely keeping over the plants. When the plants are approaching full size a light dressing of nitrate of soda raked into the soil is used to push them along and check any tendency to button. Lettuce is usually grown in the frames between the plants while small.

Dr. A. Oemler,* of Savannah, Georgia, says: "If this most delicate and most valuable member of the Brassica family, would 'carry' more safely at locations suitable for its cultivation, it would be one of the most important crops for the truck farmer. Although so situated, I have abandoned its culture, notwithstanding I have netted as high as $24.75 in New York per barrel for it, and the heads or 'curds' have sold at a gross average of thirty-seven cents each. Sometimes, however, it would continue to arrive in such bad order as not to be worth shipping. For the past two years its culture for the Northern market has been mainly confined to Florida. Coming so much earlier there, it is not exposed to heating in transit. The

---

* Dr. Oemler is the author of an excellent work entitled "Truck Farming in the South." His farm is on Wilmington Island, in the mouth of the Savannah River.

best varieties are Extra Early Dwarf Erfurt, the
Snowball, and the very large growing Algiers. It
should be marketable in March and April. The
seed therefore should be sown in the latitude of
Savannah about December first, under glass, and
the plants transplanted about January tenth."

Dr. Charles Mohr, of Mobile, Alabama, writes:
"From my own experience I judge that this vegetable does not succeed as well in the southern part
of this state as in its central and more northern
parts. I have seen it raised of good quality in the
gardens of Montgomery, and in the greatest perfection in the highlands of north Alabama at an
elevation of about 500 feet above the Gulf—at Cull-
man, in a somewhat light loamy soil, well supplied
with stable manure. In that locality the seeds are
sown by the end of February in a cold frame, to
allow protection of the young plants from frost,
and the plants are transferred to the open land by
the middle of March. They arrive at their perfection
during the first half of the month of May. Another sowing is made during the first week of
March to furnish a crop during the early part of
June. In that locality this vegetable is raised only
to meet a very limited home demand. My in-
formant at Montgomery, who raises only a supply
for his own use, writes: 'I have raised cauliflower here with success for a series of years, some

of the heads weighing six to seven pounds. The soil of my garden is a light sandy loam, requiring heavy manuring, and frequent irrigation of the plants toward the time of heading; it cannot be said to be exactly suited to this vegetable. I get my seed (the White Snowball) from Peter Henderson, of New York, sow in December in hot-bed, transplant as soon as large enough to a cold frame, and transplant as soon as danger of frost is over, say about the first part or middle of March, to the open ground, which has been well prepared and manured with stable manure. I cultivate the same as for cabbage, and the crop matures about the first of May.'

"One of the most successful market gardeners and truck farmers in this vicinity [Mobile], says: 'We have cultivated cauliflower for a long series of years, but find it much less profitable than the raising of cabbage; first, on account of its tenderness, making it liable to be injured in transportation to distant markets, and second, by reason of repeated failure of the crop in consequence of the too early advent of spells of hot and dry weather at the opening of the warm season. We sow in November in cold frame, keep well thinned out under glass until about the 20th of January, then transplant to the open ground, cultivating well with frequent watering if the weather should be dry. If the months of April and May are dry and hot the crop results in a failure, from which, in our dry and thirsty soil, no irrigation will save it. In favorable seasons we have fine results, raising heads from ten to sixteen inches in diameter. In the perpetually damp and inexhaustibly fertile soil of the alluvial lands in the Mobile River delta (marshes drained by ditching) the cauliflower is raised in the greatest perfection, and is ready by Christmas time for the home market, bringing fancy prices. In such localities the early varieties, particularly the Early Paris, are used, the seed being sown in August. Outside of these marshes the early varieties are not grown, as they produce only small and meagre heads. Among the later varieties we find Algiers and Lenormand the best, buying the seed from Vilmorin in Paris.' "

Mr. J. N. Whitner, in his work on " Gardening in Florida," recommends Early Snowball, Extra Early Paris, and Extra Early Dwarf Erfurt. The seed is sown in boxes in autumn and protected from beating rains, and if sown before the middle of October the plants are also protected from the direct sun during the middle of the day. The main crop is planted out before the first of November, and harvested the following spring. In the northern portion of the state the plants are sometimes injured by the cold in winter. The crop is not yet extensively grown in that state. In regard to suitable soil, Mr. Whitner says:

"In this state almost every truck farmer has some low rich spot of bottom, lake or river margin suitable for the production of the cauliflower. It must, however, be well drained land, and no matter how fertile it may *seem* to be naturally, a liberal supply of manure will more certainly insure handsome flower heads."

Mr. Frotzer, a New Orleans seedsman, says of the cauliflower:

"This is one of the finest vegetables grown, and succeeds well in the vicinity of New Orleans. Large quantities are raised on the sea-coast in the neighborhood of Barataria Bay. The two Italian varieties are of excellent quality, growing to large size, and are considered hardier than the German and French varieties. I have had specimens brought to my store, raised from seed obtained from me, weighing sixteen pounds. The ground for planting cauliflower should be very rich. They thrive best in rich, sandy soil, and require plenty of moisture during the formation of the head. The Italian varieties should be sown from April till July; the latter month and June is the best time to sow the Early Giant. During August, September and October, the Lenormand, Half Early Paris and Erfurt can be sown. The Half Early Paris is very popular, but the other varieties are just as good. For spring crop the Italian kinds do not answer, but the Early French and German varieties can be sown at the end of December and during January, in a bed protected from frost, and may be transplanted into the open ground during February and as late as March. If we have a favorable season, and not too dry, they will be very fine; but if the heat sets in soon, the flowers will not attain the same size as those obtained from seeds sown in fall, and which head during December and January."

In the *Texas Farm and Ranch*, H. M. Stringfellow, of Hitchcock, Galveston County, gives an account of his success with American grown (Puget Sound) seed of Henderson's Snowball cauliflower. He says:

"After two years careful trial. I have found this seed every way superior to the original imported stock, good as that was, for our hot climate. The plants are much more robust, make equally as compact but larger heads, and what is most remarkable, they mature here fully two weeks or more ahead of the imported seed. Nearly every plant will make a marketable head, and they always sell for fully double as much as cabbage.

"These American seeds begin to head about the first of November, and are nearly all gone by

Christmas, which gives ample time to get the crop off in any part of Texas.

"The cauliflower is emphatically a fall vegetable and seems to require for its perfect development a gradually decreasing temperature. The seed should be sowed from the first to the fifteenth of July, in a frame. Make the ground very rich, and if you use salt, which I consider almost an essential for this crop, turn it under deeply at the first plowing. In fact, salt and potash had better be deeply worked into the soil always, as it will not do for either to come in contact with the roots of a newly set plant.

"Until recently I have always thought that it would injure a plant to set it in soil to which cottonseed meal had been lately applied. But experiments made in the last few weeks prove that it is not only not injurious, but that cabbage plants grow off with wonderful vigor when the meal was applied the day before the plans were set.

"It will pay to subsoil for cauliflower, in order to give them all the moisture possible, though they will stand a drouth in the fall equally as well as a cabbage."

In this connection may be mentioned the following account of cauliflower growing at Durango, Mexico, sent to the *Gardener's Chronicle* in 1853: The writer says: "Of the culinary vegetables,

none excel the cauliflower, which attains such a size
that a single head measures 18 inches to 2 feet in
diameter, and makes a donkey load. The gigantic
cauliflower is not distinct from our European
species, but is solely produced by a cultivation
which necessity has dictated. Being one of the
Northern vegetables that degenerate or bear no
seed if not annually procured from Europe, it is
propagated by cuttings. After the heads are
gathered the stubs are allowed to throw out new
shoots, which are again planted and have to grow
two years, producing the second, the enormous
heads."

The following from Woodrow's "Gardening in
India," (4th edition, Bombay, 1888), contains
many interesting points of suggestive value for the
the extreme South:

"Cauliflower, being a delicate plant, always
needs great care and attention in its cultivation,
but much less care is necessary in this country
than in Europe. The soil most suitable is a rich
friable loam, such as occurs in the black soil of the
Duccan, the alluvial tracts in the basin of the
Ganges or Nerbudda. Thorough working of the
soil is necessary, and in stations where the market
price of cauliflower is usually over four annas per
head, as is the case in many parts of Southern
India, the crop is well worth extra care in the

preparation of the soil. This process should be begun shortly after the rains, when the soil is easily plowed or dug. It should then be turned up roughly to a depth of a foot or fifteen inches. A month later the clods should be broken with the mallet or clod crusher, and the plow put through the ground a second time. When the soil has weathered a few weeks, the scarifier or cultivator should be run over it once monthly until May. At that time good decayed cow dung or poudrette should be spread one inch deep, and any close growing crop which is not valuable, such as *sunn*, *tag*, *chanamoo*, or *Crotolaria juncea*, should be sown to keep down weeds and encourage the formation of nitric acid in the soil, which has been proved to be effected to a greater extent under a crop than on bare soil. During dry weather in August the crop should be pulled up and the ground plowed or dug and the crop buried in the trenches to act as green mauure, and the land prepared for irrigation.

The seed-bed should be prepared by thorough digging and mixing about an inch in depth of old manure; wood ashes and decayed sweepings having a quantity of goat or sheep dung in it is well suited for the seed-bed at this season. Cow dung is apt to have the larva of the dung beetle in it—a very large caterpillar which destroys young plants by eating through the stem under ground. The bed having been thoroughly watered, the seed may be sown broadcast or in lines, and covered with a quarter of an inch of fine, dry, sandy soil, and shaded from bright sunshine. When the seedlings appear, gradually remove the shade. The most convenient form of bed is not more than four feet in width, the length being sufficient for the ground to be planted. One ounce of seed is sufficient for a bed fifty feet square, which will give sufficient plants for an acre if the seed is good. Sowing should be made once in ten days, from the middle of August till the end of September. If the garden has been neglected, or the district remarkable for the quantity of grubs that yearly come out in August, spread a considerable part of the garden with a thick coating of stable litter or dry leaves and burn it, prepare the seed bed in the middle of the burnt space, and soak two pounds of saltpetre in water for one hundred square feet, and water the bed with it for at least two weeks before sowing the seed. When the seedlings have acquired about five leaves, and the ground to plant is ready, lift the young plants gently on a cloudy day, and plant them out two and one-half feet apart each way. If bright sunshine comes out, shade the newly moved plants with broad leaves, and water them daily with the watering pot for a few days, besides irrigating sufficiently to keep the soil moist. Afterwards, hoeing, picking grubs and replacing the losses from the seed-bed must be attended to.

The selection of sorts is a serious matter in cauliflower culture, because many sorts grow only to leaves in some climates, and great loss has been met with by some people in consequence of getting the wrong variety. The variety known to English seedsmen as Large Asiatic, has established itself in the Northern Provinces, where a good head of cauliflower is procurable in December for one-half anna. In Bombay the same would cost ten times that sum. The seed of this variety is remarkably cheap in the districts it bears seed in. From Shajehanpore I bought large quantities at Rs. 2 per pound, while the price of seed from England was Rs. 2 per ounce. This sort is perfectly reliable when properly cultivated, but it is considered inferior in flavor and delicacy to English sorts, and its season is very short. It appears to run to seed when January comes, at whatever time it may have been sown, while English varieties come into use from the beginning of December to the end of February according to the date of sowing.

Among European varieties, success will generally be met with by sowing Early London and Walcheren. The different Giant and Mammoth varieties advertised in seedsmen's catalogues should

6

be grown as extras, and if one is found to suit the soil and climate of a particular station, it may be grown more extensively afterwards; my experience with those varieties has not been happy."

THE PACIFIC COAST.

Fine early cauliflowers are grown in California under irrigation, and marketed as far east as Chicago. Oregon and Washington include a large area adapted to cauliflower growing, and this favorable territory extends northward into Alaska. The cool, moist climate of the Upper Pacific coast resembles that of England, where cauliflowers are so extensively grown.

There are few good markets yet in this region, but the rapid growth of the cities which exist affords promise of a large future demand for this vegetable, which is likely to come into more general use as it becomes better known.

Professor E. R. Lake, of the Oregon experiment station, states that some parts of the Oregon coast are well adapted to the cauliflower, but that other interests and lack of transportation facilities have thus far prevented its cultivation for market, the bulk of the crop sold there coming from California. He adds that the Chinese in the vicinity of Portland cultivate this vegetable, but that their peculiar methods are not yet understood.

Some ten years ago experiments were begun by one of our seedsmen in raising cauliflower and cabbage seed on the alluvial tide lands on the shore of Puget Sound. These lands, after being diked and drained, proved to be remarkably well adapted to the growth of the cauliflower and its seed. Others have since engaged in growing these seeds in the same region, and the business is assuming large proportions. An account of this enterprise may be found in the chapter on Seed.

CHAPTER VI

INSECT AND FUNGUS ENEMIES.

The insect enemies of the cauliflower are the same as those which attack the cabbage and other related plants. The four here mentioned require to be specially guarded against. In preparing these notes I am indebted to Mr. L. O. Howard, of the Department of Agriculture, at Washington, for essential aid.

FLEA BEETLE (*Phyllotrea striolata*, Fabr).—This insect, also known as the "ground flea" or "Jack," seldom attacks the plants except while growing in the open ground, and is most troublesome in warm, sheltered situations. A safe preventive, therefore, is to grow the plants in beds or frames elevated about three feet from the ground. The objection to this method, aside from the extra labor involved, is the necessity of almost daily attention to see that the soil does not dry out. A supply of water must be conveniently at hand if this method is used, and it is desirable also, to prevent the beds drying out too quickly, to have the earth at least eight inches deep. In hot-beds this insect is seldom troublesome, being probably repelled by the fumes from the manure used. When the seed is sown in the open ground, as practised by many large growers, an extra quantity should be used to ensure against almost certain loss of some of the plants by the flea beetle. The soil should be rich and fine, so that the plants will pass the critical stage as quickly as possible. Sowing radish seeds with the cauliflower is practised by some, as this seed costs but little, and the radishes, coming up first, are attacked by the fleas, which, to some extent, saves the cauliflowers. When the fleas appear, almost any kind of dust will keep them in check somewhat. Lime and ashes are used, but plaster, which adheres to the leaves better, seems equally good. I have had good success with rancid fish oil, mixed as thoroughly as possible with water and sprayed upon the plants. An emulsion made of the oil, in the same manner as hereafter described for kerosene, would enable it to be used to better advantage. A decoction of tobacco, or fine tobacco dust, are standard remedies for this insect.

Cut Worms.—Cauliflower plants being fully twice as valuable as cabbage plants, and it being of more importance to have them started at the proper time, it is necessary to give greater care to protect them from cut worms. Absolutely clean land contains no cut worms, but such land is seldom used on which to plant cauliflower. Sod land, which is generally used, is nearly always full of cut worms. A multi-

tude of remedies have been proposed for this pest,
but few of them are of much value. The worms
are most abundant and destructive in the latitude
of New York during the month of May. Fortu-
nately, cauliflowers are usually set out either earlier
than this, for the early crop, so that they become
well established and out of reach before their depre-
dations seriously begin, or else, for the late crop,
they are set toward the last of June, after the
worms have begun to pupate, and are no longer
troublesome. Until recently, digging and killing
the worms by hand seemed to be almost the only
practical remedy. Of late years, trapping the
worms under bunches of grass or cabbage leaves,
scattered over the ground preparatory to setting
the plants, has been successfully resorted to. An
improvement upon this method, recommended by
the Entomologist of the United States Department
of Agriculture, is now in use, and gives excellent
satisfaction. It consists in poisoning with Paris
green the leaves used to trap the worms, so that
there is no need to collect and kill the worms by
hand. A good way to do this is to spray with
Paris green, in the usual way, a patch of young
clover, then cut it and scatter it in small bunches
over the cauliflower field a day or two before setting
the plants. For the protection of a few plants in
the garden, an effectual preventive against cut-

worms is to surround the stem with a cylinder of paper or tin. This need not touch the plant. One should expect to lose some plants, however, by cut worms, and be prepared with good plants to fill the vacancies.

CABBAGE MAGGOT (*Anthomya brassicæ*, Bouché).—Dr. J. A. Lintner, State Entomologist of New York, says of this insect: "This is probably the most injurious species of the *Anthomyiidæ*, as its distribution is very extensive, both in Europe and America, and it has shown at times such capacity for multiplication as to cause the entire destruction of cabbage crops. It commences its attack upon the young plants while yet in the seed-bed and continues to infest them, in several successive broods, until they are taken up in the autumn. The larvæ operate by consuming the rootlets of young plants, and by excoriating the surface and eating into the rind of older ones, or even penetrating into the interior of the root. When they abound to the extent of seriously burrowing the stalk the decay of the root frequently follows in wet seasons, and entire fields are thus destroyed."

The same insect attacks the turnip, cauliflower, and probably other plants. A closely related species is very injurious to the radish. The presence of the insect most frequently becomes manifest upon the cauliflower about two weeks after the plants are set out, and is recognized by the plants ceasing to grow, and wilting or assuming a bluish appearance. Such plants should be at once re-moved, together with the earth immediately sur-rounding the root, and fresh plants which have been held in reserve set in their places. The only satisfactory remedies are preventive ones. The seed-bed should be composed of soil taken from the woods, or at least from some place where no cabbages or similar plants have been grown. But the most important precaution is to avoid growing the crop year after year upon the same ground, especially after the insect has made its appearance.

The following remedy, given by Francis Brill, in his pamphlet on "Cauliflowers," is worthy of careful trial. Mr. Brill says: "The ravages of the root maggot have made the growing of early cauliflower, and even early cabbages in many sections, almost an impossibility, but there is a remedy, when the maggot has attacked the roots of the plants, which may be known by a tendency of the leaves to wilt and droop in the heat of the day, very much the same as when affected by club root. Dissolve Muriate of Potash (analyzing 45 per cent. actual potash) in water in the proportion of one tablespoonful to the gallon; or double the quantity of Kainit or common potash salts (13 per cent. actual potash). Apply this directly to the roots, about one gill to each plant, whether seemingly affected or not, for the maggot will have done much harm before the plant will show it, repeating the application as occasion may seem to require. In sections where these maggots have been prevalent it will be well to make a solution of half the above strength, and when the plants are nicely started apply in the same manner as a preventive. Care and judgment must be used not to overdo the matter, thereby killing the plants as well as the maggots. Experiment a little at first."

H. A. March, of Washington, says: "The best thing that I have found for the maggot is a *poor* grade of sulphur, sulphur before being purified, that *smells very strong.* Sprinkled over the plants it seems to drive the fly away."

CABBAGE WORM (*Pieris rapæ*, Koch).—The imported cabbage worm, now known all over the country, is the most troublesome enemy which attacks either the cabbage or cauliflower, and the most difficult one with which to deal. It seldom wholly destroys the crop, and is generally a little less destructive after a few years than it is at first, being kept in check by its natural enemies. It never disappears, however, and its numbers cannot be materially diminished for any length of time by artificial means. Among the partial remedies in use are the following:

1. Catch the butterflies with a net when they first appear in spring, before they have laid their eggs. This may keep the insect in check for a year or two when it first makes its appearance, as the butterflies are comparatively slow fliers, and may be caught without much difficulty by a spry boy, especially in the morning when the air is damp.

2. Early in the season keep the young plants excluded from the butterflies, and the whole place free from everything else of the cabbage tribe, except one or more patches of rutabagas or rape, on which the butterflies will lay their eggs. This piece is to be then plowed under.

3. Hand pick the worms from the plants after they are set out, for the first one or two hoeings, or until the worms become very numerous.

4. Spray with kerosene emulsion, made by using two gallons of kerosene, one-half pound of common or whale oil soap, and one gallon of water. Dissolve the soap in the water, and add it, boiling hot, to the kerosene; then churn, while at least warm, for five or ten minutes, by means of a force pump and spraying nozzle, until the mixture loses its oiliness and becomes like butter. When used, dilute one part of the emulsion with about fifteen of water, and spray it upon the plants by means of a force pump and spraying nozzle. This emulsion

is also excellent for the cabbage louse and many other insects. In the report of the United States Department of Agriculture for 1883 may be found a description and figure of a suitable spraying apparatus.

5. Pyrethrum, one ounce to four gallons of water; or, better still, mixed one part with about twenty parts of flour and applied while the dew is on, is an effectual remedy.

6. Hot water, at 130° Fah., will kill the cabbage worms and not injure the leaves. Boiling water, placed in sprinkling cans and taken directly to the field, will be about the right temperature by the time it can be applied. Experiments with a few plants may be needed to enable one to get just the right temperature to kill the worms and not injure the plants.

7. Take half a pound of London purple to thirty pounds of finely pulverized dust of any kind, the finer and drier the better; mix thoroughly, passing all through a meal sieve. Dash a small pinch into the heart of the plant, so that it will settle as dust on all the leaves. Repeat after every rain. Half a pound will serve for one application over forty acres. Store any that remains in a very dry place until again wanted.

8. Professor Gillette, of Colorado, finds the best remedy to be Paris green, thoroughly mixed, one

ounce with six pounds of flour, and dusted lightly over the plants while the dew is on.

FUNGUS DISEASES.

There are several parasitic fungi which are more or less destructive to the cauliflower at different stages of its growth. The principal diseases of the cauliflower due to fungi are the following:

STEM ROT.—This is an old disease, which attacks the cauliflower, cabbage and other vegetables in wet seasons. It has received various other names, such as "consumption," "humid gangrene," etc. Professor Comes,* who has studied this disease in Italy, believes it to be the same as the "humid gangrene" which occurs in Germany, and which is there attributed to the parasitic attack of the fungus known as *Pleospora Napi.* He finds this

---

* *Bull. Soc. Bot. France, 1886 (Rev. Bib.,* p. 128). La cancrena del Cavolo Fiore (*La gangrene humide du Chou-fleur*) par M. le Professor O. Comes (*Atti del R. Instituto del incorraggiamento alle Scienzie naturali.* —Estratta dal Vol. IV, 3ª serie, degli Atti Academici, 1885). [The Humid Gangrene of the Cauliflower.]

"A disease which attacks the crops of cauliflower around Resina and at Torre del Greco, near Naples. The roots of the diseased plants remain sound, or at least appear so, but the subterranean parts of the stem are more or less seriously affected; the bark is disorganized, the wood situated beneath it more or less decomposed, and the pith destroyed for a variable length

and other fungi present, but does not himself consider them the direct cause of the disease, which he
attributes solely to the abundance of manure and
moisture in the soil, and an excess of water in the
plant, at a time when it is subject to sudden
changes of temperature. Beyond a doubt, however, the real cause of the disease is the presence
of one or more fungi, whose development is favored

Upon microscopic examination the vessels are found
filled with gum. M. Comes recognizes in this disease
all the symptoms of the affection which has been designated under the name humid gangrene. He thinks that
it is the same disease which, by German authors, is
attributed to the parasitism of *Pleospora Napi*, Fuckel,
or to its conidiferous form, *sporidesmium excitosum*,
Kuehn. But he considers the presence of these parasites as an accessory phenomenon, as well as that of
Cladosporium and *Macrosporium Brassicae*. In his
opinion the true cause of the alteration of the cauliflower is the humid gangrene, that is to say, a gummy
degeneration and putrid fermentation of the tissues,
caused by the abundance of manure in the soil and the
excess of water in the plant at a time when it is subject
to sudden changes of temperature.

"This disease is not confined to cauliflowers; it is
common in all garden vegetables, and is of the same
nature as that which attacks tomatoes and which was
. described by this author in the same journal in 1884."
[This disease is also mentioned by Victor Paquet, in his
"Plantes Potagers" (London, 1846, p. 243), where it is
attributed to stagnant moisture].

by the damp weather. The subject requires further study.

In this country this disease has been reported from Michigan, New York, Maryland and Florida. On Long Island, in 1889,* the cauliflower crop was almost entirely destroyed by this disease, which was attributed to the heavy rains at the time the plants were heading. Some fields were a total loss, and from the best fields many of the heads spoiled before they reached the market.

No satisfactory remedy is known for the disease. The avoidance of damp soils and locations would be of some benefit, but is hardly practicable with the cauliflower. Wide planting is practiced on Long Island in order to diminish the tendency to the disease. It undoubtedly has this effect to some

---

* *Country Gentleman*, 1889, p. 769, (from the *Port Jefferson Times*, Sept. 27):

" Close upon the heels of a partial failure of the potato crop through rotting comes the news from various points on Eastern Long Island that the cauliflower crop has almost totally failed through the same cause. In Manorville the crop has not sufficiently developed in some of the fields to warrant picking, and in Mattituck and east of that place the rotting will result in an almost total loss. In a few cases there is not yet any indication of rot, but the farmers are afraid to tie the plants up lest rotting ensue.

" In East Moriches, Orient, and the near vicinity, the yield will not be of sufficient value to pay for plowing

extent, by permitting a more free circulation of the air, thus drying up the moisture on the plants and thereby lessening the opportunity for the germination of the spores. The increased distance may also diminish the chance of the spread of the spores from plant to plant. When this disease appears upon the early crop in hot-beds or cold frames it may be kept somewhat in check by giving as much air as possible, and taking care not to apply water to the leaves.

DAMPING OFF.—This is usually due to a species of Pythium (a fungus closely related to that which causes the potato rot), which attacks the young plants soon after they germinate. The remedy is, to give the plants plenty of air until their stems become strong enough to resist its attacks. An

---

the ground, not to speak of the other expenses which have been entailed. Through the Hamptnos careful observations failed to reveal scarcely a single successful crop.

"Last Saturday Henry T. Osborn, of East Moriches, tied up 2,000 heads and on Monday he cut enough to fill 30 barrels. He let them lie in his barn over night, and the next day not a barrel of them was fit for shipment to market.

"George Cooper, of Mattituck, planted seven acres of cauliflower which he thinks will prove a total loss. And so on the reports come from many East End farmers. The recent heavy rains are generally assigned as the cause of the failure."

additional precaution sometimes employed is to grow the plants in pans or small boxes and water them only by setting these in a tank of water of nearly the same depth, allowing the water to soak into the soil, but not touch the plants. The disease is seldom troublesome on plants grown thinly in the open air. If it makes its appearance, water thoroughly, but not too often, and sprinkle dry sand over the seed-bed among the plants.*

BLACK LEG OR MILDEW.—This is a disease which attacks the stems of young plants which are being wintered over. It is undoubtedly due to one or more species of parasitic fungi, but I do not find that the subject has been studied. Doubtless the rupture of the bark by alternate freezing and thawing gives the fungi an opportunity to attack the plant. The disease is prevented and kept in check by keeping the seed-bed dry. An occasional dressing of sand, lime, wood-ashes or rubbish of any kind, is useful.

---

* A series of articles upon "damping off" may be found in the *American Garden* for 1889, pp. 347-9.

CHAPTER VII.

CAULIFLOWER SEED.

With no vegetable is it more important to have good seed than with the cauliflower, and in none is there a greater tendency to deteriorate. On this account less dependence is to be placed upon named varieties than in some other cultivated plants, and greater need is required to secure carefully selected strains. Owing to peculiarities of soil, climate and season, and the different degrees of care given by the different growers, seeds of the same variety may be better from one source than from another. On this account, when a variety is found adapted to one's needs it is well to use the same variety, and obtain it from the same source year after year.

Cauliflower seed is mostly grown in Europe, chiefly in Holland and Germany, to some extent in Italy and France, and less in England. One variety, the Large Asiatic, seeds abundantly in Northern India. There are a few localities where the seed is successfuly grown in the United States.

In Europe the dwarf early varieties are chiefly grown in the north, and the large late varieties at the south. In the south the seed is most easily grown, and southern seed brings the lowest price.

McIntosh states that cauliflower seed seldom ripens in Scotland. In England, as I have said, it is grown to a limited extent, but not so much as that of broccoli. The seed plants are there selected in June, at the time of heading, and allowed to stand until the seed matures. Mr. Dean states that his Early Snowball produces in warm, early seasons better seed in England than anywhere else. Loudon, in his "Encyclopædia of Gardening" (5th Ed., 1827) quotes Neill, as saying that "Until the time of the French Revolution, quantities of English cauliflower were regularly sent to Holland and the low countries, and even France depended on us for cauliflower seed. Even now English seed is preferred to any other."

A later English writer states that the English prefer Dutch seed and the Dutch English seed.

Most of the seed now used in England, as well as nearly all of that sold in this country comes from Holland, France and Germany. The climate, especially of Holland and North Germany, is particularly favorable for the production of fine strains of seed, especially of the dwarf early varities.

McIntosh ("Book of the Garden," 1855, Vol. II, p. 116) says: "Our best cauliflower seed is imported from Holland, and for its quality we have much greater reason to thank the better climate than the growers, who are not over particular in the matter, as Dutch cauliflower seed is sure to sell."

The Mediterranean varieties are generally large, and require for the most part too long a season to be popular and successful in this country. As dwarf varities have been produced, the cultivation of this vegetable in Europe has extended farther north. As already stated, when the cauliflower was first cultivated in France the island of Cyprus was the only place where it was known to seed, and for a time the plant was known in England under the name of Cyprus Colewort.

Although most of the seed used in the United States is still imported, American grown seed appears to give good satisfaction and is moderate in price. Professor W. J. Green, of the Ohio ex· periment station, who tested Puget Sound seed in 1889, reported as follows: "The most remarkable examples [of the superiority of Northern grown seed] are found in the Puget Sound cabbage and cauliflower seed, which show great vitality and consequent vigor in growth of plant. We have received numerous samples grown in that region by H. A. March and A. G. Tillinghast, brother of Isaac Tillinghast, the seedsman. These seeds were very large, full of vitality, and the plants uncommonly vigorous. At transplanting time the plants were nearly twice the height of others of the same variety, while the difference in color was very marked. This robust habit continued to manifest itself during a greater part of the season, but as maturity approached, the variation was less and less marked, until at last the others had caught up, and there was no perceptible difference." No change in time of maturity or habit of growth was noticed.

Mr. Brill, of Long Island, states that to secure seed there it is best to winter over the partially headed plants in a cold frame or cellar, and set them out early in the spring. The summers are so warm there, however, that except in particularly favorable seasons but little seed forms. Several excellent early varieties have originated on Long Island, and there is reason to believe that hot, changeable climates, though unprofitable for the growing of seed, are particularly favorable for the production and maintenance of early sorts able to head in hot weather.

It is perhaps for this reason that England, Denmark, and Central Germany have produced more early varities than Holland, France and Italy. The dry calcareous soil of some parts of England appears to be particularly favorable to the production of early varieties.

In the vicinity of Boston, cauliflower seed has been grown to some extent, especially the variety known as Boston Market, which was formerly very popular there. James J. H. Gregory writes me under date of March 3d, 1891, that he raised 60 pounds of seed of the Boston Market from 500 plants, where from the same number of plants of the Snowball and Extra Early Erfurt, grown under precisely the same conditions, he obtained less than a great spoonful. The seed was raised on an island used expressly for that purpose.

It is a custom in England and Holland, where the season is too short for the seed to ripen perfectly, to diminish the number of seed-stalks on a plant by cutting out the centre of the head. The flower-stalks require to be supported by stakes, and when the seed is nearly mature, to be guarded from birds. A plaster cat is recommended as a good scare-crow, especially if its position is changed every few days, so that the birds will continue to think that it is alive.

Cauliflower seed, as is well known, is smaller and inferior in appearance to cabbage seed, and always contains a considerable proportion, which is shrunken and worthless. This poor seed is removed from the crop as much as possible before it is sold. This shrunken condition arises from the fact that a large share of the flowers fail to set, and many of the pods only partly fill. Shrunken seed is no indication of inferiority of variety, in fact rather otherwise, for the most compact heads, being the most deformed from a structural point of view, give the least amount of good seed. Still, it is not necessarily true that the highest priced seed is always the best and most economical to use. A new variety, until it becomes well established, requires rigid selection, and this so reduces the amount produced that a high price can be obtained for all that is grown. An older variety, on the other hand, which has become so well established, and comes so true that nearly every head is perfect and will furnish good seed, can be supplied at a cheaper rate and may for a given purpose be equally good. As a rule it may be said that the newest and highest priced seeds are too expensive to use on a large scale, and the cheapest seeds are inferior in quality. One should not judge of the value of a variety wholly by the price at which its seed is sold. Most of the high priced varieties are dwarf kinds, which are becoming more and more popular in this country, but which produce comparatively little seed. .

Our varieties of cauliflowers have all been developed by means of selection. Desirable features have either been aquired by gradual selection through successive generations in a given locality; or some sudden variation has been preserved and perpetuated. Climate, as already stated, has had much to do in developing certain peculiarities. The varieties of Italy, France, Holland and Germany have in each case certain features common among themselves which can only be accounted for by the influence of the particular climate in which they are grown. It is, therefore, useless to attempt to maintain these characters wholly unchanged in other climates. Hardiness, earliness, certainty of heading, protection of the head by leaves, and shortness of stem, can all be increased by selection, but, as they are all likewise influenced by climate, the selection is more effective in some climates than in others. The varieties of the south of Europe are as a whole characterized by a long period of growth, tall stems, great vigor and hardiness, and by having the leaves inclined to grow upright and protect the head.

The cauliflower crosses readily with the cabbage and other varieties and species of the genus Brassica. It does not usually flower at the same time, however, as other members of the genus, so the difficulty is not usually great in keeping it pure.

In France the cauliflower has been crossed artificially with cabbage, turnip and rutabaga, in the attempt to obtain varieties of greater hardiness. Numerous peculiar forms were the result of these crosses, some of which were good cauliflowers, said to be of increased hardiness, but none of them have found their way into general cultivation. One of these, owing to a cross with the turnip, acquired the flavor of that vegetable. A full account of these crosses may be found in the *Revue Horticole* for 1880.

The following remarks, by Mr. A. Dean, of England, on a case of apparent crossing in the cabbage tribe will be read with interest:

"A very pretty conical-headed plant of a Colewort was allowed to run to seed, but nothing else of the same family was known to be in flower for a distance of at least several hundred yards. The produce was saved and sown, and has been furnishing food for the table during the past winter, but what a progeny! Some were reproductions of the seed parent, but larger, and proved very handsome early cabbages; others were very fair Coleworts; others bad examples of Cottager's Purple Kale, others Green Kale, while others resembled sprouting Broccoli, both green and purple. One plant was an example of the once popular Dalmany sprouts, and there were many other plants that admitted of no classification. It is probable that bees, which travel long distances, had somewhere found some sprouting in Broccoli flower and had brought pollen from those to the Colewort plant in question."

Spontaneous variation has given a number of curious forms of cauliflower, including one with several heads in the place of one, and another in which the head is flattened sidewise, like the garden cockscomb. These forms have not been cultivated.

Cauliflower seed contains on an average about 7,000 seeds to the ounce, of which about one-half usually germinate, a much smaller per cent. than in cabbage. Long Island growers estimate two ounces of seed to the acre as a safe amount for the small varieties and an ounce and a half for the late varieties.

It was formerly a common belief, especially in England, that old seed would be most likely to produce good heads. There is little evidence to support this belief, and just as little ground for the more recent belief held by some that old seed is particularly liable to produce loose worthless heads. Like all other seed cauliflower seed ought to be as fresh as possible; fresh seed always germinates best and gives the most vigorous plants. Seed two or three years old, however, is generally satisfactory, and it will often grow successfully at double that age.

"CAULIFLOWER SEED GROWING ON PUGET SOUND."

By H. A. March, Fidalgo Island, Puget Sound, Washington, in *Rural New Yorker*, 1888.

"I am told by very good authority that cauliflower seeds had never been grown in the United States as a field crop to any extent until we made a success of it here on Puget Sound. In the first place a very cool, moist climate is necessary to cure [secure] seeds at all. That climate we have here on our low flat islands lying in the mouth of the Gulf of Georgia. We often have heavy fogs in the night, and always dews equal to a light shower every night all summer long. The first expense attending the raising of cauliflower seed is quite heavy. The soil must be a rich, warm loam facing the south, and it will be all the better for having a clay subsoil. We must have the land underdrained once in twenty feet, the drains being three feet deep, to give us a chance to work early in the spring, and also to take off the surplus water when we come to flood the land in July.

"To prepare the land for the crop we start in September. After the fall rains have softened the soil, plow, harrow, roll, harrow again, then replow and work it again, until the soil is as fine as an onion bed. Now we throw it into ridges, six feet apart, and it is ready for work in early spring. For manure we sow 2,000 pounds of superphosphate and ground Sitka herring, equal parts of each, to the acre. With two horses and a Planet, Jr , cultivator we work the ridges until they are nearly level. By using two horses we straddle the ridge, and save tramping it where our plants are to go.

"To get the plants, we sow the seeds about September 1, in rather poor soil, giving them plenty

of room; the rows being a foot apart and the seeds
sown thinly in the rows.   This gives us stocky and
hardy plants, which, we think, are less liable to
damp off when transplanted.   About November 1
we transplant the plants into cold frames, six
inches apart each way, as we wish to keep them
growing a little all winter.   The glasses are kept
on at night and through heavy rains.   In case of a
cold snap, we cover the glasses with mats; but that
is not often necessary, for we seldom have a temperature colder than 16° above zero.   Everything
depends on good plants and an early start in the
spring, for we raise two crops the same season, and
an early frost on our unripe seed is sure to ruin the
crop.   Now, to set the plants out and make them
grow from the start, a line is stretched along one
of these flat ridges, a boy goes along, and with a
three-foot marker marks the spots for the plants; a
man follows with a hoe and makes a hole, about the
size of a quart dish, to receive each plant.   During
the winter we have gathered up 200 or 300 tomato
and oyster cans, melted off the tops and bottoms,
leaving tubes about five inches long by three or
four across.   Now, armed with a light wheelbarrow
with a wooden tray, containing from 50 to 75 of
these cans, we go to the cold-frame (having well
soaked it with water the night before); take a can,
set it right down over the plant; press the can into

the soil about two inches, and, with a light shove
to one side, lift the plant without disturbing the
roots; fill our tray and start for the field; run the
barrow between two rows and set a can and plant
in each of the holes just made.   A boy follows with
a watering pot containing *warm* water, and pours a
gill into each tube, which softens the soil so that
the tubes can be lifted right out, leaving the plant
standing in the hole.   We brush a little dirt around
the plant, and firm it with the blade of the hoe.

"Now we have our plants set, and not one ever
wilts in the hottest spring day.   In two or three
days the cultivator is started and kept a going once
a week until the heads begin to form.   We hand-
hoe three or four times, besides fighting insects.
The cabbage maggot is our worst enemy.

"When the flowers commence to bloom out or
form heads, is the most particular time.   A man
who thoroughly understands what a perfect cauliflower is, must now go through the field every two
or three days and examine every head, and if there
is any sign of its growing in quarters, or if a leaf
is growing through the head, or if there is any
looseness in its growth, the heads are staked and
cut for market.   For, as like produces like, it will
never do to get seed from an inferior head,
especially in the case of cauliflowers; for the seeds
from these are more apt to run wild than any seed

I ever grew.   We usually set a Fottler cabbage in the place from which the poor plant has been cut, and it makes a fine head by fall.

"By the middle of June we have the field clear of all inferior heads, and their places filled with late cabbages.   About this time all the heads saved for seed are 'sponging out' preparing to throw their seed-stalks.   Now is our time to help them.   On the upper side of the field, we have wooden water tanks, each holding about 20,000 gallons of *warm* water.   The water is run into the tanks in the middle of the day through flat open troughs, which heat it up to about 70° Fah.   It is taken through canvas hose over the field, and the soil is soaked to the subsoil.   Now our underdrains come into play, for all of the surplus water is drained off in about three days, and we can start the cultivator.   We cultivate close up to the plants.   If we break the leaves off it doesn't matter, for they fall off any-way as soon as the seed stalks start.   This watering gives the plants new life and they start off for a second crop, or become biennials the first year. The watering and cultivation are kept up once in 10 days until the seed-stalks are so large that they cannot be run through without breaking the plants. The seed ripens from the middle of September to the last of October, according to how good a start was made in the spring.

"The expense and trouble are not over yet. The seed is ripening about the time our rainy season sets in, and we don't see the sun once a week on an average, so that our seed must all be dried by fire heat. Our dry-houses are 30 x 20 feet, and 18 feet high with 2 x 6 inch joists running across the houses in tiers, on which we hang the seeds for drying. A brick furnace is built in the middle of the house, with the flue running through the roof.

"We usually make three cuttings. As soon as the pods on the center stalks begin to turn yellow, and the seed a light brown, we make our first cutting. From one to three plants are put in a pile and tied with binding twine. The bundles are taken to the dry-house on wheelbarrows, made with racks on purpose for carrying the seeds. A cloth is spread over the rack to catch any shelling seeds. A man carries about 100 bunches at a load and passes them up to a man in the house who hangs them on nails driven for the purpose. The seed is allowed to hang a few days to thoroughly ripen before firing up. We aim to keep the heat in the top of the house at about 80° until the seed and stalks are dry.

"The bundles are now taken down and laid upon a cloth where they are crushed by walking on them. Grain sacks are then filled with the stalks and pods.

as full as they will tie up, and the contents are thrashed in the sacks with a flail. The seed is then sifted from the stalks and taken to the fanning-mill, and after putting it through the mill two or three times, we set the boys to rolling it. For this purpose we have a board two and a half feet long by one foot wide, with thin strips nailed on the sides to keep the seeds from rolling off. A boy sits down on a cloth with a pan of seed by his side, and holds one end of the board in his lap, while the other end rests on the cloth. He puts a handful of seed on the top end of the board and gently shakes it. All of the sound plump seeds run off on to the cloth, while the shriveled seeds, bits of stalk, dirt, weed seeds, etc., remain on the board. A smart Indian boy will clean ten pounds a day, at a cost of 50 cents and his board. Now the seed is sacked in double cotton sacks, holding about ten pounds each, and is ready for market."

In a subsequent paper the same writer said, in answer to inquiries upon the subject, that the cauli-flower and cabbage readily mixed, but that there was little danger of their doing so in his locality, as the cabbage was nearly out of flower before the cauliflower began to blossom. To make the matter certain, however, boys were sent to every neighbor-ing cabbage patch to clip off all straggling late blossoms that remained. Only one variety of cauli-

8

flower, or strains of one variety, is grown by him for seed in any one year.

The following letter from the same writer explains itself:

"FIDALGO, Washington, April 3, 1891.

"MR. A. A. CROZIER, Ann Arbor, Mich.

"*Dear Sir:*—Your letter of inquiry received. In answer would say, I am the original cauliflower raiser in the Puget Sound country. In 1882 I discovered that by wintering the plants over in cold-frame, and keeping them growing all winter, those that were transplanted *without wilting* would form heads, and then throw seed-stalks in time to form seed before frost, if they were continually wet with tepid water after heading. The first seed that was put on the market was sold by Francis Brill, River-head, L. I. Since then I have furnished some of the largest firms in the country with seed, and the seed has given perfect satisfaction. There is a secret in raising good seed that I don't care to give away. Several of my neighbors have tried to raise the seed, and I believe some of it has been put on the market, but it has proved inferior for the want of skill in knowing *which heads* to seed from, as all heads will not do to seed from, even though they may appear perfect to an inexperienced eye. It's skilled labor that produces No. 1 seed.

"I enclose you my circular, with reports from growers and dealers, also quite a few from the experiment stations. I have a large number that I have not printed, as they came too late for this year. The business has grown from a few pounds in 1882 to nearly 300 pounds in 1890. I think in the near future, that Puget Sound will grow all of the cauliflower seed that will be grown in the country. Cabbage seed is also grown to a large extent. I raised about two tons last year, and there probably will be ten tons raised on Puget Sound the coming summer.

"Cabbage and cauliflower are grown to a considerable extent both in Oregon and Washington, though California sends our first to this market.

"You ask me for an account of my Early Perfection or "No. 9." It was a *sport* or a "stray seed," found among some Erfurt Earliest Dwarf imported seed, and being the first in the field to form a head by over a week, I naturally saved it for "stock seed," and as it propagated itself perfectly, and was perfection itself, I named it Early Perfection. I am not aware of another by the name of Perfection on the market—never saw it in the seedmen's catalogues. Early Padilla and Early Long Island Beauty, by Brill, are the same; they originated with me, are a selection from *Erfurt Large*, and are *early* and *large*.

"All of Tillinghast's Puget Sound cauliflower seed has been grown by me. I have also grown all that Francis Brill has put on the market.

"D. M. Ferry & Co.'s Early Puritan originated with me, from a sport of Henderson's Snowball. I sold them the stock for two years.

"Yours Truly,

H. A. MARCH."

CHAPTER VIII.

VARIETIES.

The varieties of cauliflower differ among themselves less than those of most other vegetables, and
their characters are less firmly fixed. Their
tendency to degenerate, especially under unfavorable conditions, and the readiness with which they
may be improved by selection, has given rise within
recent years to numerous so-called varieties, some
of them but slightly differing from those from which
they originated. These have frequently received
the names of the seedsmen who first sent them out.
Many of these seedsmen's varieties have dropped
out of cultivation, as well as other varieties which
have appeared from time to time, but which have
not possessed sufficient distinctive merit. Some
varieties, from not having been kept up to their
original standard, have reverted to those from
which they sprang, or become so like them that
their names have come to be regarded as synonyms.

Nevertheless, all such names have been brought
together in the following catalogue, and all the
obtainable information given concerning the varieties which they represent. The testimony given
is sometimes contradictory, either from want of

proper observation on the part of the writers quoted, or from differences in the seeds sold under the same name. This is necessarily somewhat confusing to one who is looking up the merits of a variety, but it will form a better basis for judgment than would a mere descriptive list, without reference to dates or authorities. It is practically impossible to make a satisfactory classification which will include all the varieties, and they have therefore been arranged here in alphabetical order, as being most convenient for reference. Nearly all of the most popular varieties have, however, characters sufficiently distinct so that they can be easily recognized. Some have short stems, others long ; some are early, others late ; some have upright leaves, others drooping; their color varies from grassy to bluish green; the heads vary from snow-white to cream-colored, and in two or three varieties classed with the cauliflowers they are reddish or purple, as in some of the broccolis. The form of the head varies from flat to conical.

Most of our varieties have come from a few stocks whose characters, as well as those of their descendants, seem to have been largely determined by the locality in which they originated or have long been grown. The Algiers, Paris and Erfurt groups are examples. In each of these groups there is a series of varieties, differing mainly in size and earliness.

In the Erfurt group the production of early varieties has been carried farthest, owing doubtless to the character of the climate, as well as the greater skill employed in their selection. The early varieties, particularly of this group, are characterized by having comparatively small, narrow and upright leaves, and a rather short stem. A partial list of varieties, arranged in the order of earliness, follows the catalogue.

ADVANCE, see *Laing's Early Advance.*

ALABASTER.—Introduced to the general public by Johnson & Stokes in 1890. In their catalogue for that year these seedsmen say: " Our *Early Alabaster* was originally a sport from the finest German strain of the selected Dwarf Erfurt, one extra fine head appearing some ten days in advance of any other in the crop of one of the largest and most expert cauliflower growers on Long Island in 1881. The seed of this was carefully saved by him, and from it our stock has been brought up."

The seed of this variety has all been grown on Long Island, and it was all taken by Long Island gardeners until 1889, at which time there were said to be hundreds of acres of it in cultivation in Suffolk County, where it originated. [See Frontispiece.]

ALGIERS, (Probably includes *Large Algiers* and *Large Late Algiers*).—Vilmorin, in 1883, described

Algiers as follows: "Extremely vigorous, stronger and better developed than the Giant Naples, [Veitch's Autumn Giant]; leaves very large, undulate, almost curly, of a very deep and reflective glaucous green; stem large and strong, rather tall; head remarkably large, fine and white. In habit of growth it approaches the Half Early Paris, but in time of maturity it agrees with the varieties of Holland and England. It is especially adapted to open-air culture in a warm climate."

M. May, of France, placed it in 1880 just before Giant Naples in maturity, with a little shorter stem and little less ample foliage. He said: "Late, but of gigantic size; leaves large, long and numerous, of a glaucous green, and surrounding well the head, which becomes as large as those of our native varieties, and is snow-white and exceedingly fine. Specially suited to warm climates. In our country it may be sown in September, and gathered the following August."

Rawson, a seedsman of New York, said in 1886: "A large and very popular late variety, and one of the very best for the market. This variety is largely grown for the New York market. It is one of the largest in cultivation, and always sure to head." Frotzer, of New Orleans, describes it as a French variety of the same season as Lenormand Short-stem, but a surer producer, having taken the place

there of other second-early kinds since its introduction. At the Ohio experiment station it proved
unsuited to the climate. A writer in the *American
Agriculturist* for 1889 stated that this variety was
formerly largely grown in Suffolk County, Long
Island, but that for the past two or three seasons
it had done poorly, and would not be grown in the
future. Its large size required the plants to be set
four feet apart.

ALLEAUME (*Early Alleaume, Dwarf Alleaume*).—
This variety, originated by an intelligent market
gardener of Paris; was, according to the originator,
one of the best for cultivation under frames. Cultivated there in the open ground, that is to say,
sown in June and planted out in July, it has given
remarkably good results. It is a little below medium
height, and has a very short stem. Its oblong
leaves are of a light grayish green. The head is of
medium size, very white, fine grained, of first
quality, and early. It is a variety of great promise.
This is the statement of the editor of *Revue Horticole* in 1884. In 1888, Mr. Sutton, of England,
calls it a distinct, dwarf, compact, French variety,
having creamy-white heads, and coming in after
Sutton's Favorite. In 1890, Vilmorin quotes it as
a very early dwarf, short-stemmed variety, especially good for forcing.

In 1885, W. A. Burpee offered an " Extra Early

Alleaume," which he described as "stem very short, leaves long, *entire* or *very little lobated*, of a grayish-green color, forming a close protection to the head, which is large, fine grained and pure white." This is probably the same variety as above.

ALMA (*Waite's Alma*).—Hackett sells this as a new English variety of large size, firm, and surpassing in excellence the Walcheren. There are, however, a variety named Alma, probably the same, growing at Paris in 1857 (see *Jour. Cent. Soc. Hort. France*, 1857, p. 422). In 1865 Waite's Alma was considered by some to be merely the Early London, and by others to be the same as Walcheren; at least, seeds of these two varieties had been sent out for it.

AMERICAN.—Seed of a very early variety bearing this name was sent by William Ingell, of Oswego County, New York, to the editor of the *Country Gentleman*, in 1861. Mr. Ingell, who named the variety, does not state whether he grew the seed or not. In 1889, Bailey's "Annals of Horticulture" contained the name "American," with *American Beauty* as synonym.

ANCIENT LENORMAND, see *Lenormand*.

ASIATIC (*Early Asiatic, Large Asiatic, Large Late Asiatic, Dur d' Angleterre*).—These seem to be substantially one variety, the terms "early" and

"late" being in this, as in some other cases,
applied by different seedsmen to the same variety,
when, as in this case, it is of intermediate season.
Since the introduction of such extremely early sorts
as the Extra Early Erfurt, this and other mid-
season varieties are more often called "late." The
Asiatic seems to have originated from the Early
London, of which it is regarded as merely a
stronger growing and later variety. The first mention I find of it is in *Hovey's Magazine*, in 1845,
where Large Asiatic and Walcheren are called the
two most noted varieties. In 1849 the same magazine states that it was sent out by the London
Horticultural Society. In 1850 a writer in the
Gardener's Chronicle mentions this and Walcheren
as his two favorite varieties. In 1854, J. D. Browne
describes the Large, Late Asiatic in the report of
the United States Department of Agriculture as
larger and taller than Early London.

In 1855 this variety is mentioned in the American
edition of "Neill's Gardener's Companion" as having
recently come much into use. As this edition was taken
from the fourth Edinburgh edition, the actual date
here referred to was probably much earlier. Three
other varieties, scarcely differing in character, are
mentioned—the Early, Late and Reddish-stalked.
The Large Asiatic is now extensively grown in
Northern India, where it seeds freely, but has a

short season, and is not considered as delicate or fine in flavor as the ordinary English varieties.

AUTUMN GIANT, see *Veitch's Autumn Giant.*

BALTIC GIANT.—In Burpee's "How to Grow Cabbages and Cauliflowers" (1888). Mr. J. Pedersen, of Denmark, gives the following account of this variety: "A new variety of large, late cauliflower, originated in these northern regions, and which I propose to name Baltic Giant, is very hardy, of robust growth, and produces very large and solid dazzling white flower-heads. A friend of mine writes from the Baltic island of Bornholm that in mild seasons he has left this splendid late variety in the open ground as late as Christmas, only protected by a leaf or two bent over the heads." The variety is being tested in this country by W. A. Burpee & Co.

BERLIN DWARF.—Rawson says: "In earliness, size and quality it resembles the Snowball." Gregory, in 1890, makes the same statement.

BEST OF ALL.—An early variety mentioned in *Gardening Illustrated*, 1885, p. 438.

BLACK SICILY (*Large Black, Dwarf Early Violet Broccoli*).—Vilmorin says: " In growth and appearance this variety somewhat resembles Algiers. Stem rather tall, leaves very large, broad and much crumpled, almost curly; differs from all other cauliflowers in the color of its head, which is violet, and with a grain much coarser than in other varieties, while it is sufficiently close, solid and large. Not very late; always grown in the open air, and ready to commence cutting in September." Mentioned in *Bon Jardinier*, in 1859, as one of the three principal Broccolis, with which it is generally and properly classed.

BOSTON MARKET (*Improved Early Paris*).—This variety, which has now gone out of existence, was formerly extensively cultivated around Boston, where it originated by continued selection from the Early Paris. In the *American Journal of Horticulture*, for 1869, p. 92, is a figure and description.

BURPEE'S BEST EARLY.—An improved type of Dwarf Erfurt, named and introduced by W. A. Burpee & Co. in 1886, after, as they say, sixteen years selection by one grower. It is said to be of dwarf, compact growth, with a short stalk, and large, solid, nearly globular heads, very early and certain to head.

The Dingee & Conrad Company sell the same variety.

At the Ohio experiment station in 1889, this variety was regarded as probably the same as Large Erfurt, rather large, and a few days later than Early [Extra Early] Erfurt, but quite as good in other respects. At the Colorado station, in 1888, "Burpee's Earliest" was noted for its large leaves and white, compact heads. It headed ten days later than Henderson's Snowball.

CARRARA ROCK.—An extra selected strain of Erfurt, said by Wm. Elliott & Sons, of New York, to be the earliest and surest variety to head.

CARTER'S DEFIANCE (*Early Defiance*).—Gregory considers this a fine variety for forcing or very early use.

CARTER'S DWARF MAMMOTH.—An early variety, coming in just after Carter's Defiance. Plant dwarf, head very large, perfect in form and of fine color.

CARTER'S EXTRA EARLY AUTUMN GIANT.—A variety said, in 1889, to have large, close, white heads, both flower and leaf being less coarse than those of Autumn Giant.

CARTER'S MT. BLANC, see *Mt. Blanc*.

CHALON PERFECTION.— A variety mentioned in *Gardener's Monthly*, in 1886. Said to be as white as snow, almost as smooth as ivory, and to make good heads in soil of moderate fertility. Probably the same as Early Dwarf Chalon, which see.

CHAPEL (*Chapel's Cream*).—Catalogued in Bailey's "Annals of Horticulture," in 1889.

CLARK'S CHAMPION.—An imported English variety mentioned in *Vick's Magazine* for 1887, p. 52, as being a little later than Snowball and Vick's Ideal.

CYPRUS. — Said by Wolfner and Weisz, of Vienna, in 1888, to be a beautiful early sort. It is an old Holland variety.

DANISH SNOWBALL.—Offered by Vaughn, in 1891, who says he has tested it for two seasons, and finds it a good, extra early sort.

DEAN'S EARLY SNOWBALL.—This, the oldest, and for a long time the most popular of the Snowball varieties, has now been displaced in this country by Henderson's Snowball and other early sorts. It is often said to be earlier than Early Dwarf Erfurt, but at the Chiswick trials, in 1876, it did not prove to be so. A writer in the *Garden*, for 1880, places it third on the list of early varieties, placing Carter's Extra Early Defiance first, and Veitch's Extra Early second. It appears to be fully as dwarf as the earliest Erfurts, and to have a little larger head. It has been said, even by the introducer, to be the English duplicate of the Early Dwarf Erfurt, but there is no doubt of its distinctness from that variety, as was afterwards recognized. There was another German variety, however, name not given, at the Chiswick trials referred to, which was reported to be identical with Dean's Snowball. Mr. Dean says: "The Snowball may be told by one unfailing test, viz.: when the heads begin to burst into flower, they become suffused with a pretty purple tint."

This variety was introduced into England in 1871, by Mr. A. Dean, from Denmark, where it was largely cultivated. It is still one of the best early varieties, especially for hot weather and light soils. Mr. Dean states that it is about the only variety of which seed can be grown in England, and he considers English-grown seed of this variety the best.

DICKSON'S ECLIPSE, see *Eclipse*.

DREER'S EARLIEST SNOWSTORM.—Henry A. Dreer, in 1890, says in his catalogue: "The earliest and best of all for forcing. It is dwarf, with short outer leaves, and can be planted two feet apart each way; always sure to make large, fine heads earlier than any other, and is the market-gardener's favorite. This variety must be kept growing constantly, as it will not stand a check at any period of its growth." In 1891, he writes that this variety is a strain of Extra Early Erfurt, the seed of which is grown at Erfurt, Germany.

At the New York experiment station, in 1888, it produced heads fit for use eighteen days later than Henderson's Early Snowball, and Earliest Dwarf Erfurt.

DWARF ERFURT (*Extra Early Erfurt, Early Dwarf Erfurt, Extra Early Dwarf Erfurt*).— These names all refer to practically the same variety, which is usually sold in this country under the name of Extra Early Dwarf Erfurt, and is now the most popular early variety grown. It is similar in habit to its parent, the Early Erfurt, but more dwarf, and the leaves smaller and more upright, allowing the plants to be set closer together. The heads are close and well formed, but do not remain solid long, owing largely to the hot weather in which they are generally formed. The best seed comes from Erfurt, Germany, but as the variety rapidly deteriorates, there is great difference between the selected and ordinary stocks.

Johnson & Stokes say, in their catalogue for 1890, that their extra selected Early Dwarf Erfurt is distinct from the Early Dwarf Erfurt. Burpee calls his Extra Early Dwarf Erfurt "the finest of all early cauliflowers." He, as well as some other seedsmen, sell different qualities, "extra selected," "true," numbers "one" and "two," etc. French-grown seed sells for about half the price of German seed.

At the Chiswick trials, in 1876, where all known varieties were grown, the Early Dwarf Erfurt proved to be the earliest variety grown. It is best grown as a summer variety, being rather tender for a late crop, though sometimes used.

M. May, in the *Revue Horticole*, for 1880, describes this variety as follows: "Early Dwarf Erfurt. Very early, with light-colored, short, upright, spoon-shaped leaves, which surround the head

9

well, but do not cover it. The head is well rounded, very regular, of remarkable whiteness, and very fine and close. It readily attains a diameter of fifteen to twenty centimeters [about five to seven inches]. This variety is especially adapted to forcing, as its small size permits it to be readily cultivated under glass. The best times for sowing it appear to be at the beginning of spring and the end of summer. One may also sow it in September to obtain a crop in April and May."

Mr. J. Pedersen, of Denmark, speaks as follows of this variety in Burpee's work on "Cabbages and Cauliflowers:" "The success with cauliflowers depends greatly upon the right choice of varieties. This year, for instance, we have in this country suffered from drouth to an extent not known of for the last score of years, and yet I have seen a surprisingly grand field of cauliflowers, of an improved strain of the Early Dwarf Erfurt variety, grown in a stiff clayey soil, very dry in the surface, not in the best state of cultivation, and without any artificial watering whatever. The roots of the plants were 'puddled' when planted out; that was all. I do not believe that seven per cent., perhaps not five, of said field of thirty or forty thousand plants failed to make fine, large, solid, beautifully white and typical heads. Other varie-

ties have either utterly failed, or made stunted, im-
perfectly developed heads."

At the New York experiment station, in 1882,
the Extra Early Dwarf Erfurt was slightly earlier
than the Early Dwarf Erfurt, and produced double
the proportion of good heads.

The Ohio experiment station, in 1889, reported
as follows: " The varieties or strains most highly
recommended are Early Puritan, Early Padilla,
Long Island Beauty, Early Sea Foam, Early Snowball and Vick's Ideal.   These all appear to be
nearly identical with Early [Extra Early] Erfurt,
and may be considered as strains of that variety."

As the Dwarf, or Extra Early, Erfurt has furnished
a large share of the varieties now popular in this
country, the following list of Erfurt varieties will
be useful for reference.   The first three are in the
order of earliness; the others (descended from
Dwarf Erfurt,) being alphabetical:

Early Erfurt Mammoth.

EARLY ERFURT.

Dwarf Erfurt.

     Alabaster (Johnson & Stokes).

     Berlin Dwarf.

     Best Early (Burpee).

     Carrara Rock.

     Gilt Edge (Thorburn).

     Ideal (Vick).

Imperial.

Lackawanna (Tillinghast).

La Crosse Favorite (Salzer).

Landreth's First.

Long Island Beauty (Brill).

Model (Northrup).

Padilla (Tillinghast).

Prize? (Maule).

Puritan (Ferry).

Sea Foam (Rawson).

Small-leafed Erfurt.

Snowball (Faust).

Snowball (Henderson).

Snowball (Thorburn).

Snowstorm (Dreer).

Snowstorm? (Pearce).

EARLY.—At the New York experiment station in 1888, a variety called "Early," from the English Specialty & Novelty Seed Co., was the only one among nine varieties which failed to head. The Early London White is sometimes known as "Early."

EARLY ALLEAUME, see *Alleaume.*

EARLY DEFIANCE (Sutton), see *Carter's Early Defiance.*

EARLY DUKE.—Mentioned as one of the best four early varieties for Central France in the *Annales de la Sociètè d' Horticulture de l' Allier* for 1852. See **Lefevre.**

EARLY DUTCH.—An old variety, described by Vilmorin as follows: "A large hardy variety, suitable for field cultivation. Stem long and rather slender; leaves elongated, but very large, of a grayish green, somewhat undulated. This is one of the varieties in which the side of the leaf is bare at the base for a considerable distance. The head is hard and solid, yet very large. It is a half-late variety. In its original country it does better than the French varieties and it is cultivated on a grand scale around Leyden. Large quantities are shipped to England, where it is found in the London markets, together with cauliflowers from the coasts of France, and especially Great Britain. The name Dwarf Holland, which is given to this variety in Germany, can only be explained by comparison with other Holland varieties. In comparison with the French varieties it is tall."

EARLY DWARF CHALON.—Vilmorin catalogues this as "new" in 1889, and says: "Stem very short, head rather large, grain white and very close. Specially recommended for open air culture." See Chalon Perfection.

EARLY DWARF FORCING (Sutton).—No description.

EARLY DWARF SURPRISE.—An early variety from Vilmorin, which headed well at the New York experiment station, in 1884.

EARLY DWARF VIENNA.—Said by Wolfner and Weisz, of Vienna, to be an old superior sort, still grown for the first and second crop.

EARLY ERFURT (*Erfurt, Large Erfurt, Large Early White Erfurt, Late Erfurt*).—This is still a popular variety, but less hardy and less valuable as a late sort than the improved varieties from the south of Europe; and as an early sort it has been displaced by its offspring, the Extra Early Erfurt, and the newer varieties derived from that. The heads of the Early Erfurt are large and fine-grained but more inclined to be open and leafy than those of Early Paris. It is a little earlier than that variety. Vilmorin describes the Early Erfurt as follows: "Very early, distinct, and valuable, but difficult to keep pure. Below medium height; stem rather short; leaves oblong, entire, rounded, and slightly undulated; of a peculiar light grayish green, which, added to their form and their rather erect position, gives to the plant an appearance somewhat resembling that of the Sugar Loaf. Head very white, fine grained, rapidly developed, but not inclined to remain long solid."

The *Bon Jardinier* mentions the Erfurt, in 1859, among the novelties as the earliest variety then known, being two weeks earlier than Salomon (Early Paris) and very suitable for forcing on account of its straight, upright leaves and earliness.

EARLY ERFURT MAMMOTH (*New Erfurt Dwarf Mammoth* [Burr], *etc*)."—Burr in 1886, said: "A recent sort with large, clear white flowers, of superior quality. The plants are low and close, and generally form a head, even in protracted dry and warm weather. It appears to be one of the few varieties adapted to the climate of this country." This form of Early Erfurt has not been kept distinct.

EARLY FAVORITE.—A variety without description is sold under this name by A. B. Cleveland & Co. See also Haskell's Favorite.

EARLY GERMAN.—"A new variety advertised in English Catalogues:"—(*Mag. of Hort.*, 1838, p. 50).

EARLY LA CROSSE FAVORITE.—John A. Salzer offers this as earlier than Henderson's Early Snowball, and "the earliest, finest, whitest and most compact grown." At the Ohio experiment station in 1889 it was apparently the same as the ordinary large Early Erfurt. Mr. Salzer writes me that it is a distinct type of his own originating from the Early Erfurt.

EARLY LEYDEN, see *Walcheren*.

EARLY LONDON (*London Particular, Fitch's Early London, Early English, Large Late*).—An old sort, still quite popular in both the United States and England. Vigorous and hardy, with large, abundant, deep-green, undulated foliage; stem rather tall, but shorter than that of Early Dutch; head well formed and somewhat conical. Formerly the main variety grown as an early crop about London, but there are now varieties much earlier.

Vilmorin regards it as the same as Early Dutch, which is evidently an error.

EARLY LONDON MARKET (Gregory), see *Early London.*

EARLY LONDON WHITE (Sutton).—An early form of Early London, cultivated some twenty years ago, but now seldom heard of.

EARLY PADILLA (*Long Island Beauty*).—The Early Padilla was named and sent out by Tillinghast in 1888, who says that it is a sport from Henderson's Snowball which originated on one of his seed farms on Padilla Bay, Puget Sound, in the State of Washington. Mr. H. A. March, of Fidalgo, Washington, who states that he grows all of Tillinghast's Puget Sound cauliflower seed, says that Early Padilla originated with him from the Large Erfurt, and was named by him the American, and so published at first in one of his circulars. Seed of the same was also supplied by him to Francis Brill, of Long Island, who named it and sold it as Long Island Beauty.

At the New York experiment station in 1888, the Early Padilla equalled in earliness Henderson's Snowball, and was slightly surpassed by Extra

Early Dwarf Erfurt, while the variety obtained as Long Island Beauty was the earliest of the nine early varieties on trial. At the Ohio experiment station in 1889, Long Island Beauty was called a very perfect strain of Early [Extra Early] Erfurt.

EARLY PADILLA.

Gregory said in 1890: "Of the thirteen varieties of cauliflower raised in my experimental plot in 1888, every specimen of the Long Island Beauty made fine heads, and the heads averaged larger than any other sort. It is among the very earliest

. . . . Mr. Brill calls it, 'absolutely and unequivo-
cally the best cauliflower in the world.'"

EARLY PARIS (*Tendre de Paris, Salomon, Petit
Salomon*).—An excellent sort, more largely grown
for a fall crop in this country in the past than any
other variety.   Intermediate in season between
Half Early Paris and the newer Extra Early Paris.
Described by Vilmorin as follows: "Plant small,
rather tall; leaves comparatively narrow, nearly
straight, a little deflexed at the extremity, and
slightly wavy at the border; head of medium size,
quickly formed, but remaining firm but a short
time.   This variety is particularly suitable for the
summer crop; sown in April or May it heads in
August or September."   In this country, when
used as a fall crop, no complaint is made of the
heads not remaining firm.   Sown in May in the
latitude of New York it heads in September and
October.   M. May, of France, describes this variety
as follows in the *Revue Horticole* for 1880: "An
early variety grown by gardeners in the outskirts
of Paris.   It has nearly the appearance of the Half
Early Paris, but is smaller, with a little shorter
leaves, which are more narrow and upright.   It is
sown in September, and wintered over under hand
glasses on a bank composed of manure from an old
hot-bed and exposed to the south.   The crop is

then gathered during May. It may also be sown in March and gathered in July."

Victor Paquet, in his work on Vegetables (*Plantes Potagers*), published at Paris in 1846, gives a full account of cauliflower culture and says: "We cultivate two distinct varieties, *tendre* and *demi-dur*. The sub-varieties *gros* and *petit* Salomon are sorts of the *tendre*."

Richard Frotzer, of New Orleans, catalogues the Extra Early and the Half Early, but not the Early Paris.

Mr. Gregory, of Massachusetts, states that most of the seed sold in the United States as Early Paris is really the Half Early. In a recent letter he says: "The Early or Half Early Paris is now about dead, the various strains of Extra Early Erfurt, such as Snowball, Sea Foam, etc., having taken its place." There is no doubt, however, of the Early and Half Early Paris being two varieties. The former, which has so long been a favorite in the Northern States may still be relied upon, though in many cases, as stated, it is being displaced by the Extra Early Paris, and particularly by the Extra Early Erfurt and varieties derived from it.

EARLY PICPUS.—Catalogued by Vilmorin in 1889 as a new early variety with large white heads, good for field culture.

EARLY PURITAN.—A little the earliest of four varieties at the New York experiment station in 1889, the others being Early Erfurt, Snowball, and Vick's Ideal. At the Ohio station the same year it was considered to be a strain of Early [Extra Early] Erfurt and one of the best of its class.

D. M. Ferry & Co., the introducers of this variety, write me as follows regarding its history: "The Puritan cauliflower originated as the product of a particularly early, large-headed, and dwarf-growing plant found in a large crop of Snowball during the summer of 1886. The seed from this plant was saved, and selections made from the product until a sufficient quantity was secured. It was first noticed and selected by one of the largest cauliflower growers in this country, and great care was taken in selecting and seeding the plant. It is purely American, both in origin and growth."

It appears from the letter of H. A. March, on another page, that this variety originated with him from Henderson's Snowball, at Fidalgo, Washington.

EARLY SNOWBALL.—Under this name Dean's Early Snowball is generally known in England, and it is probably the variety often sold as Snowball in this country. Henderson's Early Snowball is, however, now sold under that name by many seedsmen, and is the one sent out as Early Snowball by the United States Department of Agriculture·

EARLY WALCHEREN, see *Walcheren*.

ECLIPSE.—The first notice I find of this variety is in the *Gardener's Chronicle* for 1877 (Vol. VIII), where it is mentioned as being sent out by Dickson Brown & Tait. It is similar to Veitch's Autumn Giant, but about three weeks earlier. It is said to be a fine variety, with large heads, well protected by the leaves, and to stand drouth well. At the Ohio experiment station in 1889, the heads were invariably loose and sprangled.

ERFURT, see *Early Erfurt*.—The Erfurt varities are characterized by a light pea-green color, and stiff, more or less upright leaves.

EXTRA EARLY ALLEAUME, see *Alleaume*.

EXTRA EARLY DWARF FORCING.—Probably *Extra Early Erfurt*.

EXTRA EARLY ERFURT, see *Dwarf Erfurt*.

EXTRA EARLY PARIS.—This variety is not described by Vilmorin in his *Plantes Potagers*, but it is probably the one given in his catalogue under the name of "Extra Earliest Paris (forcing)." It is catalogued by the leading American seedsmen without description.

FAUST'S EARLIEST TRUE SNOWBALL.—H. G. Faust & Co., say in their catalogue for 1890: "Our Snowball cauliflower is undoubtedly the best in cultivation. It is the earliest grown, produces the finest snow-white heads, and its compact habit enables it to be planted closer together than any other variety."

FAVORITE, see *Early La Crosse Favorite, Haskel's Favorite*, and *Early Favorite*.

FRANKFORT GIANT, see *Veitch's Autumn Giant*.

FRENCH, see *Large White French* and *Half Early French*.

FRENCH IMPERIAL (Thorburn), see *Imperial*.

FROGMORE EARLY FORCING. — An old variety, described by F. Burr, in 1866, as follows: "Stem quite short, and plant of compact habit. The heads are large and close, and their color clear and delicate. Recommended as one of the best for forcing, as well as an excellent sort for early culture."

In 1876, a writer in the *Country Gentleman's Magazine* mentions it as the earliest variety grown, to be followed by Early London. It is now, however, but little used.

GERRY ISLAND.—A variety said by Gregory to be a very reliable header, closely resembling Early Paris. At the Colorado experiment station in 1888, it failed to head.

GIANT MALTA.—Said to be a large, fine variety, with beautiful white heads of excellent flavor. Though dwarf, it is late, requiring six months in which to develop.

GIANT NAPLES.—Described as synonymous with Veitch's Autumn Giant, by Vilmorin, in 1883, but he now catalogues it as a separate variety, similar to Veitch's Autumn Giant, but later. It is doubtless the original, of which the Autumn Giant is a slightly improved form. M. May said of Giant Naples, in 1880: "Very similar to Algiers, a little taller stem, and more fully developed foliage. Highly esteemed in Italy and Algeria. Requires the same culture as Algiers."

GILT EDGE EARLY SNOWBALL (Thorburn).—This American variety was reported by the Pennsylvania experiment station in 1888, as having done well and formed good heads, free from intermixed leaves, where nearly all other sorts failed. "It is a superior selected strain of Early Snowball which originated on Long Island and is of the same type as the best strain of imported Dwarf Erfurt." —(Johnson & Stokes, 1891).

GRANGE'S AUTUMN—A variety mentioned in the *Gardener's Chronicle*, in 1870, as earlier and inferior to Veitch's Autumn Giant.

HAAGE'S EARLY GERMAN.—Said by Wolfner and Weisz, of Vienna, to be an excellent short-stemmed variety for the open ground.

HAAGE'S DWARF.—Said by Wolfner and Weisz, of Vienna, to have large, compact heads, which keep long in good condition.

HAAGE'S NEW DWARF EARLY.—"The best for forcing."—(Frederick Adolph A. Haage, Jr., Erfurt, Germany, 1890).

HALF EARLY FRENCH (Landreth, 1886).—Thorburn, in 1891, catalogued Half Early Large French, and in previous years Half Early Dwarf French.

HALF EARLY GIANT ITALIAN.—A new variety catalogued without description by Vilmorin, Andrieux & Co., in 1889.

HALF EARLY LARGE WHITE FRENCH (Vilmorin, Andrieux & Co.).—No description.

HALF EARLY PARIS (*Demi-dur de Paris, Gros Salomon, Nonpareil*).—Valuable for a late crop in this country, and now the most popular variety in the New Orleans market. Described by Vilmorin, of Paris, as follows: "Plant medium; leaves rather large, of a deep, slightly glaucous green, surrounding the head well, and gradually reflexed from the base to the apex; border undulate and coarsely dentate; stem rather short and stout; head very white, large, and remaining solid a long time. Formerly the most extensively cultivated for the Paris market, but now giving place to Lenormand Short-stem, and several new varieties."

In the *Revue Horticole* for 1880, M. May says: "This is the variety most cultivated around Paris, because it is suited to all seasons. It may be sown: (1) In September, to be gathered in May and June, being protected during winter like the Early Paris; (2) in February, in a hot-bed, or under hand-glasses or frames, to be gathered in June and July; (3) at the first of March, also in hot-bed, to be set out in April and gathered in July; (4) finally, it may be sown in June on a border of rich mold, and set out in July, without having been transplanted. This very simple method requires frequent waterings to yield good results. The crop is gathered from September to November."

The name *Gros Salomon*, now given by Vilmorin and others as synonymous with Half Early Paris, was applied by Ribaud, in 1852, to a separate variety (*Annales de la Société d' Horticulture de l' Allier*, 1852, p. 59). For remarks on the synonym "Nonpareil," see that name.

Mr. Gregory, of Massachusetts, says of the Half Early Paris or *Demi-dur:* "This is the kind usually sold in this country as Early Paris, the true variety making so small a head as to be comparatively worthless here."—(Gregory, "Cabbages and How to Grow Them," 1870, p. 69).

HALF EARLY ST. BRIEUC (*Demi-dur de St. Brieuc*).—"Plant large and strong; leaves quite large, elongated, undulate and of a deep green; stem long; head close, solid, and remaining a long time in good condition. This variety, which is

10

extensively cultivated around St. Brieuc, from which it is exported to Paris, and even to England, is quite hardy, and is well adapted to open-air culture."—(Vilmorin).

HASKELL'S FAVORITE.—As grown at the South Dakota experiment station, in 1888, no difference was seen between this and Henderson's Snowball. Seed was sown in hot-bed April 10, the plants set out in well-manured soil May 24, and the first heads cut July 13—from which time the plants continued to head along through the season. The introducer, George S. Haskell, of Rockford, Ill., writes: "The Early Favorite we sell is a variety I found in Holland a number of years ago. It has proved a very sure header in this section of the country, and will yield more than other sorts. It is not of the 'Erfurt family,' but about half way between the Early Paris and Erfurt."

HENDERSON'S EARLY SNOWBALL.—A German variety, derived from the Dwarf Erfurt, introduced by Peter Henderson & Co., about 1878, and which has become very popular. Gregory, in 1890, said that it was not excelled by any other variety, unless it was Thorburn's Gilt Edge, and that it combined the best characteristics of Berlin Dwarf, Extra Early Erfurt, and Sea Foam. Henderson & Co. state that it is now grown for forcing more largely

than any other variety. It is sold by some seedsmen simply as Early Snowball.

W. J. Green, of the Ohio experiment station,

HENDERSON'S EARLY SNOWBALL.

says: "This justly celebrated strain of Early [Extra
Early] Erfurt is probably better known than the
parent variety. The true Henderson's Early Snowball is unexcelled, but there are other strains, and
other varieties even, that have been sent out under
this name, which are very inferior."

The stock of this variety is all controlled by Peter Henderson & Co., and is grown in Germany. Seed descended from Henderson's stock has been grown at Puget Sound, and is claimed to be as good as the original. Several other sorts, including Puritan and Padilla, have been derived from Henderson's Snowball, which often mature quite as early as this variety.

IDEAL, see *Vick's Ideal.*

IMPERIAL.—May says, in the *Revue Horticole*, for 1880: "A variety which seems to have originated from the Early Dwarf Erfurt, being a little more vigorous, and producing a little larger heads, which is without doubt a result of culture, for in head and leaf it wholly resembles the Erfurt. It is an excellent variety, employed in the same manner as the Erfurt, and deserves extended cultivation."

Vilmorin says: "This fine variety resembles the Dwarf Early Erfurt, but it is of deeper green, and every way larger. It is an early variety with beautiful white head, large and solid, and remarkable for its regularity of growth and product. When well grown it is certainly among the most desirable early varieties." Thorburn considers it one of the best for the main crop. It originated about 1870. It matured in one season eighteen days and in another thirty-two days before the Lenormand.—(*The Garden*, 1873, p. 2).

IMPERIAL NOVELTY (Landreth), see *Imperial.*

IMROVED EARLY PARIS, see *Boston Market.*

ITALIAN GIANT.—There are two or more forms of this variety in the market. For example, Vick sells "Italian Giant," Gregory, "Italian Early Giant," the Plant Seed Company, "Italian Early Giant Autumnal," Vilmorin, "Half-Early Italian Giant (new)," Frotzer, "Late Italian Giant," and Vilmorin, "Late Giant Italian Self-protecting." The early form or variety seems to be the most generally sold by our seedsmen, and is perhaps the one indicated when the simple name Italian Giant is used. Gregory calls the Early Italian Giant a "fine, large white-headed early variety." Frotzer says it is not quite so late as the Late Italian, almost as large, and in every way satisfactory. The Late Italian Giant, he says, is grown to a considerable extent in the neighborhood of New Orleans, and is the largest of all the cauliflowers and should not be sown later than June, as it requires from seven to nine months to head.

JOHNSON & STOKES' EARLY ALABASTER, see *Alabaster.*

KING, see *Sutton's King.*

KNICKERBOCKER.—An early variety with "fine large compact snow-white heads of excellent flavor."—(E. & W. Hackett, Adelaide, Australia, 1889).

LACKAWANNA.—An American variety sent out by Tillinghast, about 1884, and said to be a little larger and later than Henderson's Snowball.

LANDRETH'S FIRST.—As grown at the New York experiment station in 1885, it was equal in earliness to the Early Dwarf Erfurt, and surpassed only by Henderson's Snowball.

LARGE ALGIERS, see *Algiers*.

LARGE ASIATIC, see *Asiatic*.

LARGE ERFURT.—A name sometimes applied to the ordinary Early Erfurt, in distinction from the Dwarf Erfurt.

LARGE EARLY DWARF ERFURT (Thorburn), see *Early Erfurt*.

LARGE EARLY LONDON.—Failed to head at the New York experiment station, in 1882. In 1885 a small proportion of the plants headed; it was the latest among 38 varieties.

LARGE EARLY WHITE ERFURT.—Brill calls this the lowest grade of the Erfurt type, succeeding admirably at times, but not to be depended on, and apt to grow with small fine leaves through the heads. See Early Erfurt.

. LARGE LATE ALGIERS, see *Algiers*.

LARGE LATE ASIATIC, see *Asiatic*.

LARGE LATE WALCHEREN (Dreer), see *Walcheren*.

LARGE WHITE FRENCH.—A fine large white variety, catalogued by Gregory and others in 1890. Vilmorin calls it half-early.

LARGEST ASIATIC.—Taller and larger than the common Asiatic, but apparently no longer grown. The *Gardener's Chronicle* for 1848 mentions it as being sold by Messrs. Schertzer, of Haarlem.

LAING'S EARLY ADVANCE.—A writer in the *Gardener's Chronicle*, for 1891, p. 121, states that he has grown it for the past three years and finds it a good variety, with close white heads of moderate size, protected by many well-incurved leaves, and ready for use about five months from the time of sowing the seed.

LATE DUTCH (*Large Late Dutch*).—Sold by several American seedmen. Probably distinct from Early Dutch.

LATE LENORMAND SHORT-STEM, see *Lenormand Short-stem.*

LATE LONDON (Burpee and Ferry).—No description. See Asiatic and Large Early London.

LATE PARIS (*Dur de Paris*).—This, said Vilmorin in 1883, is the latest variety cultivated by the market gardeners around Paris. It differs from the Half Early Paris, especially in being a little later, and in having its head remain hard and solid a long time; but it is also distinguished by the appearance of its foliage, which is quite abundant, elongated, very much indulated, and of an intense green.

This variety is the least cultivated of the three generally grown at Paris. The gardeners use it only for the summer sowing to come at the end of the season. It is now being supplanted by other late sorts.

LATE WELCHEREN, see *Walcheren*.

LEFEVRE.—Said to have been one of the best four varieties for Central France in 1852, the others being *Demi-duro de Paris* (Half Early Paris), Early Duke, and *Gros Salomon*.

LE MAITRE PIED COURT.—As grown at the New York experiment station in 1885, it was rather early. Probably the same as the "Lemaitre" or Chambourcy Short-Stemmed, catalogued by Vilmorin in 1890.

LENORMAND (*Ancient Lenormand, Late Lenormand, Lenormand Extra Large, Lenormand Mammoth*).—Vilmorin said, in 1883: "It is now a score of years since the attention of the trade was called to this variety, principally because of its beauty and its great hardiness against cold. The Lenormand is in appearance but little different from the Half Early Paris (*Demi-dur*). The leaves are only a little larger. It certainly requires a little less care than other varieties, but its chief merit is having given birth to the Lenormand Short-stemmed, which is to-day one of the most generally prized,"

M. May describes and figures this variety in the *Revue Horticole* for 1880. In the *Journal of the Central Horticultural Society of France* for 1857 is a report of a committee of that society upon this variety as grown on the grounds of M. Lenormand near Paris, it having been introduced by that gentleman in 1852 from Halle, in Central Germany, where it was then largely cultivated. The committee made a very flattering report, finding the Lenormand much finer than the other varieties, Half Early Paris, Erfurt, and Alma, growing in the same field.

In this country the Lenormand was formerly a popular variety, being frequently mentioned, as long ago as 1858, with the Early Paris as one of the two best varieties. Since then it has been displaced by the following:

LENORMAND SHORT–STEM.—This variety, derived from the Lenormand, is described by Vilmorin in 1883 as follows: "The aspect of this variety is very characteristic, and enables it to be distinguished easily from all others when it is well grown. The stem, extremely short, strong and stocky, is furnished down to the level of the earth with short, large, rounded leaves, slightly undulated except on the borders, very firm and stiff, and more spread-

ing than upright; color deep green, slightly glaucous; head very large and solid. beautifully white,
and keeping in condition a long time.   This variety
is early. productive, hardy against cold and drougth,
and requires comparatively little room.   Its rapid
extention in cultivation within the last few years is
not therefore surprising."

LENORMAND SHORT-STEM.

To this it may be added that the variety is sold
by nearly all our American seedmen and is a popular variety for a fall crop, especially at the South.
Its large, solid, cream-colored heads are not however as well protected by the leaves as those of
most other medium early or late sorts.

LENORMAND'S SHORT-STEMMED MAMMOTH (*Lenormand's Extra Large Short-Stemmed*).—This appears to be a selection from the Lenormand Short-stem. It is offered under the second of the above names by Vilmorin, and under the first by Gregory and other American seedsmen.

LONG ISLAND BEAUTY (Brill), see *Early Padilla*. At the Colorado station, in 1888, seeds of Long Island Beauty obtained from Low appeared to be an inferior stock, and gave heads which were loose and yellowish. For the origin of this variety see Early Padilla.

MALTA GIANT (Burpee), see *Giant Malta*.

MARTIN'S PRESIDENT.—As grown by Mr. R. Gilbert at Burghley, England, in 1885, this variety stood the exceptionally dry season better than Best of All, Snowball, Early Erfurt, Veitch's Autumn Giant.—(*Gardening Illustrated*, 1885, p. 438).

MAULE'S PRIZE EARLIEST, see *Prize*.

MITCHELL'S HARDY EARLY.—Said by F. Burr, in 1866, to be "a new variety, boquet not large, but handsome and compact. It is so firm that it remains an unusual length of time without running to seed or becoming pithy."

MODEL.—The Northrup, Braslan & Goodwin Co., of Minneapolis, Minnesota, the introducers of this variety, say in 1891: "The history of our Model cauliflower we can give you in a few words. We have for several years been testing cauliflower seed from as many growers as posible, in order to secure a variety which we could identify with our name. We have never been fully satisfied until two years ago, when we received from a foreign grower a sample for trial. Upon testing this seed in our experimental grounds we found it so desirable that we arranged for the stock we are now selling, and which gives excellent satisfaction wherever grown. There are other varieties which produce as good heads and as early, but in our growths of this sort we have found a larger proportion of large, white, perfect heads than in any other strains we have tested."

MOHAWK WHITE CAP (Nellis).—"Rather larger and later than Early [Extra Early] Erfurt and seems to be identical with Snowball from the same firm."—(Ohio Exp. Station, 1889).

MT. BLANC.—Said by Buist, in 1890, to be one of the largest and finest for forcing, or the general crop. Stem medium; heads large, snow-white, well protected by the leaves, and of delicate flavor.

At the Oregon experiment station, in 1890, Carter's Mt. Blanc resembled Perfection in growth, but had somewhat larger heads.

NAPLES, GIANT, see *Veitch's Autumn Giant.*

NARROW-LEAVED ERFURT, see *Small-Leaved Erfurt.*

NE PLUS ULTRA.—A fine early variety, derived from the Giant Naples, having well-filled heads, often nine inches in diameter. Highly recommended by Wolfner and Wiesz of Vienna, but little grown in this country.

NONPAREIL.—In most American catalogues this is given as synonymous with Half Early Paris. Buist and Rawson catalogue it as a separate variety, and Brill mentioned it in 1872 as a distinct variety. At the New York experiment station, in 1885, a variety called Thorburn's Nonpareil matured among the half-early sorts at the same time as Lenormand Short-stem. J. M. Thorburn & Co. write me in 1891 that Nonpareil is a name which they gave to the Half Early Paris when they first introduced that variety to the trade in this country.

NORTHRUP, BRASLAN & GOODWIN CO'S MODEL, see *Model.*

PADILLA, see *Early Padilla.*

PALERMO VIOLET.—A variety catalogued by Wolfner and Weisz, of Vienna, in 1888.

PAQUES.—A variety with fine white heads, usually classed with the Broccolis. Catalogued by Vilmorin, in 1890.

PARIS, see *EarlyParis.*

PEARCE'S SNOW–STORM (*J. S. Pearce & Co's Snow-Storm*).—This variety, introduced by these seedsmen, of London, Canada, 1886, appears from their description to be a selection from the Dwarf Erfurt.

PEARL (*Veitch's Pearl*).—A good second-early sort sent out about eight years ago; said by some to be too near King in character. It seems to be no longer grown.

PERFECTION (*March's No. 9*).—Received from H. A. March, of Fidalgo, Washington, and grown at the Oregon experiment station in 1890, it was found to be equally good with Snowball, and similar in growth to Mt. Blanc, but with a little smaller head.

Mr. March writes me as follows, under date of April 3, 1891:

"My Early Perfection, or 'No. 9,' was a sport or, 'stray seed' found among some Erfurt Earliest Dwarf, imported seed; and being the first in the field to form a head by over a week, I naturally saved it for 'stock seed,' and as it propagated itself perfectly, and as it was perfection itself, I named it Early Perfection. I am not aware of another by the name of Perfection in the market."

PICPUS EARLY HARDY.—At the New York experiment station in 1885 this proved to be a large, rather early sort. Vilmorin includes it in his latest catalogue, but it is not in the American catalogues.

PRIZE (*Maule's Prize Earliest*).—An Erfurt variety sent out by Wm. H. Maule, of Philadelphia.

PURITAN, see *Early Puritan*.

RAWSON'S EXTRA EARLY SEA FOAM.—Said by Rawson in 1886 to be the best forcing variety; dwarf, very compact, with large, firm, well-rounded heads, pure white, and of the best quality. At the Ohio experiment station in 1889 it appeared to be the same as Early [Extra Early] Erfurt.

RICE'S GIANT SNOWBALL.—A late sort, which failed to head well at the New York experiment station in 1883.

SMALL-LEAVED ERFURT (*Earliest Dwarf Small-Leaved Erfurt, Narrow-Leaved Erfurt*).—This, according to Brill, differs from "Erfurt Extra Dwarf Earliest" in having very narrow, pointed leaves which grow perfectly upright, thus adapting it for close cultivation or for forcing. It grows rapidly, which adapts it for spring cultivation; and for a fall crop it may be sown later than any other variety—on Long Island usually as late as July 1st.

SNOW'S WINTER WHITE.—A late variety usually classed with the Broccolis.

STADTHOLDER.—Burr, in 1886, said, "A recent variety introduced from Holland . . . In the vicinity of London, where it is largely cultivated for the market, it is considered equal, if not superior, to the Walcheren." Vilmorin describes it as follows: "Very near Early Dutch, being distinguished mainly by being a few days later, being thus inter-

mediate between the Early Dutch and Walcheren.
The stem is a little shorter than that of other Holland cauliflowers and the leaves are more undulated
on the border." It is a good sort, but hardly equal
to Autumn Giant and some others which protect
the head better, and have now largely displaced it
in cultivation.

ST. BRIEUC, *Demi-dur de St. Brieuc.*—Said by
May in 1880 to be "a hardy, but late variety, inferior in its head to our Paris varieties, and not
very generally cultivated."—(*Revue Horticole*). At
the New York experiment station in 1885 it gave
good results.

SURPRISE, see *Early Dwarf Surprise.*

SUTTON'S FAVORITE.—Said by Sutton & Sons to
be seven to twelve days earlier than Early London,
of level and compact habit, and good to succeed
Sutton's Magnum Bonum.

SUTTON'S FIRST CROP.—Said to be the earliest to
head, very dwarf and compact, having snowy white
heads, and so few leaves that it may be planted
closer than any other kind.

SUTTON'S KING.—Said by Sutton & Sons to be
the best cauliflower for general use, coming in immediately after Sutton's Favorite. Plant dwarf
and compact, with large, firm, beautifully white
heads. Endures drouth well. Said to produce a
greater weight on a given area than any other

variety. Heads have been grown weighing 28 pounds.

SUTTON'S MAGNUM BONUM.—Sutton in 1888 says: "We introduced this cauliflower to our customers last year as the finest and most delicately flavored variety we have grown." Heads large, firm, snowy white; plant medium early, of strong, dwarf, habit and broad leaves, which "are serviceable for shading the heads."

SUTTON'S SNOWBALL.—A very early dwarf variety mentioned in the *Garden* in 1875.

TARANTO.—Offered as new by J. M. Thorburn, in 1891, and said to be very large and to resemble Autumn Giant.

THORBURN'S EARLY SNOWBALL (Thorburn, 1890). —No description.

THORBURN'S GILT EDGE.—Gregory says in 1890: "This is undoubtedly the finest strain of the Snowball variety. It is a little later and larger than the common Snowball, and can be left longer in the field without decaying. I considered it the best of all the dozen varieties raised in my experimental grounds this season."

THORBURN'S NONPAREIL, see *Nonpareil.*

THORBURN'S WONDERFUL.—At the New York experiment station in 1883 this variety matured with Veitch's Autumn Giant and Walcheren, and was larger than either of those. At the same station in

I I

1885 a variety called Wonderful, probably the same, was the latest of 30 sorts, being sown March 30th, set out May 4th, and gathered Oct. 27th.

VAUGHN'S EARLIEST DWARF ERFURT.—In his catalogue for 1891, Vaughn says that this is the highest priced and finest strain of the Earliest Dwarf Erfurt, imported from Erfurt Germany. This strain has been imported by him for several years. He remarks that many strains of Dwarf Erfurt are given special names by other seedsmen.

VEITCH'S AUTUMN GIANT (*Autumn Giant, Giant Naples, Frankfort Giant*).—No other new variety of cauliflower has attracted so much attention as this. It was introduced into England about 1869, since when it has become very popular there for a late crop and for summer. It is rather too late for the ordinary fall crop in this country, though a favorite with some growers on both the Atlantic and Pacific coasts.

It was described by Vilmorin in 1883, as follows, under the name Giant Naples, but is now sold by him as Autumn Giant: "Plant large and vigorous, stem rather tall, leaves abundant, somewhat undulated, of a deep green. The interior leaves turn in well over the head, which is very large, solid, and white. It is a late variety of the same period as Walcheren, but less hardy. At the north it can be employed for the latest crop in open air culture by being sown in April or May."

In 1884 Vincent Berthault gave the following account of this variety in the *Revue Horticole:* "This variety is still rare and little known in France. I planted it last year for trial and obtained results which were the admiration of all who saw them. It was from my small crop that I took the four which I had the honor to present to the Central Horticultural Society of France at its meeting on August 25, 1883. Some of these cauliflowers were 35 to 38 centimeters [more than a foot] in diameter, and weighed, including stem and leaves, 12 to 13 kilograms [nearly 30 pounds] which is extraordinary for this time of the year, when it is difficult to obtain cauliflowers of even ordinary size. At one time I feared that their size was to the detriment of their quality, but it has proved otherwise, and in all respects they are excellent, and as good as beautiful. In fact they are perfect.

"The general characters of the Autumn Giant differ materially from those of other varieties.

"The young seedlings become at once very tall and upright, and even after being set out and planted as deep as the first leaves they quickly assume their usual stellate appearance, and for about six weeks they are simply furnished with eight or ten long narrow leaves borne on a long stem. So up to this time the plants are not very promising, and one is tempted to pull them up; but after this the plants rapidly change in appearance; a dozen new leaves are quickly developed, and the plants take on a half-upright form which recalls that of the Half Early Paris variety. As to the head, it is more conical than flat. The leaves sometimes attain a length of 90 centimeters [nearly three feet], by 40 centimeters broad. It is then that extra care should be given. The waterings ought to be copious and frequent, especially at the time of the formation of the heads, when I apply about 10 to 15 litres of water to each head every other day. This, which certainly contributed to the good result, is how I grew my plants. I chose good soil, which I prepared during the winter, placing in the bottom of the furrow a good thickness of manure, and a month before planting, or even at the time of doing so, I spread on the surface a covering of decomposed manure, which I incorporated with the soil by means of ordinary tillage. I visited the plantation every day, not only to destroy the caterpillars, but to cover the heads with leaves, which it was necessary to look after at least every other day in order to preserve the whiteness of the heads. These attentions are indispensable if one would secure a product of first quality, free from insects. As to sowing the seed, it may be begun about the 15th of September, and the plants wintered over under hand-glasses, or in frames, to be set out in March, when heads will be obtained in July. The plants of this sowing may also be set in hot-beds in January and February, but this only in default of other varieties, for they will be too tall and spreading.

"It is in February, on a bed with mild heat and under glass, that I make my sowing to obtain plants which are to head in August and September, and which give my best returns. A final sowing may be made at the end of March or beginning of April; it matures its crop in October and November.

"My opinion of the Autumn Giant is that it is destined to play an important part in the market-gardening of the country when, probably in the near future, there shall have been produced dwarf varieties analogous to those which we already possess from other sorts."

VEITCH'S EARLY FORCING.—This variety "has small compact hearts, very close and white. The habit of the plant is dwarf and sturdy, and it is well adapted for forcing."—(*Gardening Illustrated*, 1885, p. 427). It is favorably mentioned by several writers in the *Gardener's Chronicle* for 1884 and 1885. In the *Garden* for 1882 Veitch's Early is said to be two weeks earlier than Early London.

VEITCH'S PEARL, see *Pearl*.

VEITCH'S SELF–PROTECTING.—Said by the *Gardener's Chronicle*, in 1874, to be a new variety, just tested by Mr. Veitch, much later than Autumn Giant, hardy, and very self-protecting.

VICK'S IDEAL.—James Vick says in 1890: " We introduced the ' Ideal ' to public notice in 1886, and claimed for it superiority to any other variety in the following points: Reliability of heading, size and solidity of heads, earliness, and protective habit of inner leaves." Further tests by himself and others he says substantiate these claims. The plants are said to be very dwarf, with erect outer leaves. At the New York experiment station, in 1889, it was a few days later than the three other varities on trial. At the Ohio station the same year it was considered one of the best strains of Early [Extra Early] Erfurt.

VIENNA CHILD.—Catalogued by Wolfner and Weisz, of Vienna, in 1888, at the highest price, as a fine new market-garden sort.

VIENNA EARLY DWARF, see *Early Dwarf Vienna*.

WAITE'S ALMA, see *Alma*.

WALCHEREN.—This old German variety is intermediate in character between the true cauliflowers and the broccolis, and it has, from the first, been frequently called Walcheren Broccoli. There seems to have originally been two varieties, Early and

Late. The earliest appearance of the name
Walcheren that I have seen is in an advertisement
of Walcheren cauliflower seed in the *Gardener's
Chronicle* for 1844. Since that time it has remained one of the most reliable and popular
varieties with English growers.

McIntosh, in his "Book of the Garden," in 1855,
said that it was hard to get pure seed: "The true
Walcheren is distinguished from all others by its
bluntly rounded and broad leaves, and the close-
ness and almost snowy whiteness of its heads, even
when grown to a large size." Others, before this,
state that it was sold on the Continent under the
name of Early Leyden.

Burr, in 1866, records it as synonymous with
both Early Leyden, and Legge's Walcheren broccoli or cauliflower. He describes it as resisting
both cold and drouth better than other varieties,
"stem short, leaves broad, less pointed and more
undulated than those of the cauliflower usually are."

Vilmorin described it in 1883 as synonymous
with Walcheren Broccoli, known in Holland as
Late Walcheren. He said: "The latest and most
hardy of the cauliflowers, and therefore intermediate
between the cauliflowers and the broccolis, with
which latter it is often classed. Stem high and
strong, leaves elongated, rather stiff and upright,
abundant, and of a slightly grayish green. The

head forms very late, and is fine, large, and very white, of fine close grain. The seed requires to be sown at Walcheren, [an island on the coast of Holland] in April, in order to be certain of heading before frost. If sown later it often passes the winter and heads early in the spring."

Sibley, in 1887, sold this variety under the name of Early Walcheren, though giving it the usual characters and season of the ordinary late sort. Buist, in 1890, mentions it as a favorite, very hardy, late variety. It is sold by most of our seedsmen, but is less popular in this country than in England. Sutton, the English seedsman, describes it in his latest catalogue as an "excellent mid-season cauliflower." It is less liable to button in dry weather than most other varities, but sometimes forms imperfect heads.

WEBB'S EARLY MAMMOTH.—A variety advertised as follows by Webb & Sons of Wordsley, Stourbridge, England, in *The Garden*, Feb. 9, 1878: "An excellent compact variety; stands the drought remarkably well; heads large, firm, and beautifully white. The best of all for the main crop."

WELLINGTON.—Introduced about 1860. Henderson & Co. describe it as the finest kind in cultivation; pure white; size of head over two feet in circumference, and as large as thirteen inches diameter; very dwarf, the stem not more than two or three inches from the soil, but with ample foliage; one of the hardiest varieties known, and said to withstand well the variable climate of the United States. C. G. Anderson & Sons of England, in 1880, claimed it to be earlier, white, and closer than Early London.

A writer in the *New England Farmer*, in 1871, speaks of it as larger than either Early Erfurt or Early Paris.

WONDERFUL, see *Thorburn's Wonderful*.

ORDER OF EARLINESS.

The following varieties cover the season, and are arranged in the order of earliness, as near as can be determined. Many well known kinds are omitted, and some little known sorts inserted, the only attempt being to form a scale of maturity:

Early Dwarf Erfurt.
Extra Early Paris.
Early London.
Asiatic.
Early Erfurt.
Early Paris.
Lenormand Short-Stem.
Late Paris.
St. Brieuc.
Algiers.
Veitch's Autumn Giant.
Giant Naples.
Veitch's Self-Protecting.
Late Italian Giant.
Walcheren.

NEW YORK EXPERIMENT STATION (*Geneva*).—In 1883 the following twenty-two varieties were sown April 16, and eleven plants of each variety set out May 15. One variety, however, Rice's Giant Snowball, was sown May 13, and set out June 20. Treatment was the same as for cabbage.

VARIETY.	First head in days.	No. of plants.	No. of heads.	Diameter of largest head in inches.
Algiers......................	159	6	5	9
Algerian Late..............	142	9	1	6
Berlin Dwarf...............	124	8	2	5
Carter's Defiance...........	124	7	6	–
Carter's Dwarf Mammoth....	124	6	2	9
Earliest Dwarf Erfurt......	124	10	4	7
Erfurt Early Dwarf.........	131	6	3	5
Early Dutch................	142	7	3	6
Early London	129	6	4	9
Extra Early Paris	142	3	2	9
Gerry Island	133	3	3	6
Imperial....................	119	8	7	10
Italian Giant White	175	6	1	10
Large Late London.........	128	6	5	7
Large White French........	105	8	8	6
Lenormand's Short-Stemm'd	128	5	5	8
Rice's Giant Snowball.......	152	7	1	4
Snowball	128	5	4	6
Stadtholder	128	6	5	9
Thorburn's Wonderful......	128	4	4	6
Veitch's Autumn Giant.....	128	6	3	6
Walcheren..................	128	3	3	6

In 1884, the following twenty varieties were grown. The seeds were sown in a green-house March 5 and 6, and the plants set out May 2. It appears from the table that some of the varieties called "late," formed heads earlier than others called "early." The Lenormand Extra Large was the earliest, forming its first head in 149 days, the Lackawanna heading a day later. None of the heads were extra large:

VARIETY.	First head in days.	Plants survived.	Number of heads
Dwarf Erfurt.....................	182	4	4
Early Dutch or Early London..	180	5	4
Early Dwarf Surprise..........	175	6	6
Eclipse	162	7	6
Half-Early Large White French	190	9	6
Half-Early Paris...............	197	8	7
Imperial......................	160	8	8
Lackawanna	150	9	8
Large Algiers.................	189	6	3
Large Late Asiatic............	156	4	4
Large Late Stadtholder........	—	8	3
Late Giant Italian............	154	8	8
Late Paris....................	170	4	3
Lenormand's Extra Large.......	149	7	6
Lenormand's Short-Stemmed...	161	8	6
Paris Extra Early.............	154	6	6
Sea Foam.....................	182	3	2
Veitch's Autumn Giant........	182	6	3
Very Dwarf Alleaume..........	189	8	6
Walcheren.....................	182	6	4

In 1885 the following varieties were planted in the green-house March 30, and sixteen plants of each, with a few exceptions, transplanted to the garden May 4. The plants of Algiers and Le Maitre Pied Court were transplanted May 20, and those of the Wonderful May 21. The plants were set in rows three and one-half feet apart, and eighteen inches apart in the rows. Many were destroyed by various causes, and though the places were twice reset there were many vacancies.

As will be seen, Henderson's Early Snowball (from Henderson in 1885) was the earliest, forming the first head July 8, or ninety-seven days from sowing the seed. The heads also were rather above the average in size. Extra selected Dwarf Erfurt was the second in earliness and every plant headed.

A notable fact brought out by this table is the effect of the early planting on the late and half-early varities. It might be supposed, as these varities require a long season, that this early planting would give the best results, enabling them to attain their full development. But it appears that it caused many of the plants to head prematurely when small, while it greatly prolonged the season of the variety.

VARIETY.	First head.	No. of plants.	No. of heads.	Average diameter of head.
Algiers......................................	Aug. 14	22	19	7½
Alleaume	Sept. 24	5	4	7
Autumn Giant.........	" 24	17	17	7
D'Alger	" 15	14	12	7½
Demi dur de St. Brieuc..............	" 15	11	11	7
Early Dutch (dur d' Holland)......	Aug. 25	12	8	5
Early Dwarf Erfurt (Thorburn)...	July 13	11	11	5½
Early Dwarf Erfurt (Vilmorin)...	" 13	5	4	5½
Early London	Aug. 25	16	12	7½
Early Paris......	July 25	11	6	5½
Early Picpus.................................	Aug. 5	12	10	8
Early Snowball................................	July 31	17	15	7
Extra E. Dw'f Erfurt (Hend'son).	Sept. 27	18	8	6
Extra E'ly Dw'f Erfurt (Thorb'n)	July 13	12	11	5½
Extra Earliest Paris (Vilmorin)...	Aug. 10	7	6	7½
Extra Early Paris.....................	July 25	13	6	6½
Extra Selected E'ly Dwarf Erfurt	" 21	13	13	5
Half Early Dwarf French...........	" 25	12	7	7½
Half Early Paris (Thorburn)......	Aug. 24	12	11	6½
Half Early Paris (Vilmorin).......	Sept. 15	11	11	7
Henderson's Early Snowball......	July 8	12	9	7½
Imperial........................	Aug. 10	10	8	6½
Landreth's First......................	July 13	6	5	5½
Large Early London	Oct. 27	14	4	6
Large Late Asiatic	Aug. 25	11	7	8
Late Giant Naples	Oct. 17	5	3	4
Late Paris................................	Aug. 12	10	7	7½
Late Stadtholder	Oct. 7	11	6	5½
Le Maitre Pied Court..............	Aug. 14	15	13	7
Lenormand	Sept. 15	12	10	6½
Len'm'd Short-stem'd (Hend'son)	Aug. 14	20	11	6
Len'm'd Short-stem'd (Vilmorin)	July 25	12	7	7
Purple Cape (Noir de Sicilie)	Aug. 10	12	8	6½
Thorburn's Nonpareil..................	" 14	7	6	8½
Veitch's Autumn Giant.............	Sept. 24	13	11	7½
Walcheren (Henderson).....	" 1	4	4	7½
Walcheren (Vilmorin)................	Aug. 5	6	6	7
Wonderful	Oct. 27	7	6	6

The following early varities were tested in 1888. The seeds were all sown May 10, and the plants set out June 23, two by three and one-half feet. All the varities headed well, except one called "Early," from the English Specialty and Novelty Seed Co., which formed no heads.

Variety.	Seeds from.	No. of plants.	No. of heads.	Fit for table use.
Dreer's E'st Snowstorm	Dreer.	11	8	Sept. 24
Earliest Dwarf Erfurt.	Vaughn.	9	5	" 6
Extra E. Dwarf Erfurt.	Tillinghast.	9	4	" 20
Gilt-edge Snowball.....	Thorburn.	12	10	Aug. 25
Henderson's E. Snowb'l	Henderson.	12	8	Sept. 6
Long Island Beauty...	Tillinghast.	11	8	" 14
Long Island Beauty...	Bragg.	12	11	Aug. 25
New Early Padilla.....	Tillinghast.	11	8	" 29

At the same station, in 1889, the following varieties were tested. The seed was sown in frames April 23, and the plants set out June 22. The Early Erfurt and Early Snowball were from seed grown by H. A. March, of Fidalgo, Washington.

Variety.	Seed from.	Number of Plants	Fit for table use	Number of heads	Average diameter
					Inches
Early Puritan....	Ferry.	20	Aug. 21	13	5½
Early Erfurt.....	March.	20	" 22	19	8½
Snowball.........	March.	20	" 24	20	7¼
Vick's Ideal......	Vick.	20	" 30	20	7

The season of 1889 was uncommonly favorable for the cauliflower, and it will be seen from the above table that these varieties headed with greater uniformity and from two to four weeks earlier than the same or similar varieties the preceeding year.

COLORADO EXPERIMENT STATION (*Fort Collins*).— The following report, slightly condensed, from the report of the Colorado experiment station for 1888, will be useful for comparison: "Seed of sixteen varieties of cauliflower was sown April 12 in hotbed and transplanted to the open ground May 7. They were irrigated at planting time, and on May 14 and 28, June 11, July 5 and 20, August 3 and 15 and on September 5. The area in crop was one-third of an acre and the stand nearly perfect. The plants were hoed twice and cultivated six times. The soil, a clay loam, was lacking in fertility for the best culture of the cabbage and the cauliflower. Of the varieties grown, Henderson's Snowball was the best, with the latter's Erfurt a good second. These two types, when well selected, are the only ones that can be relied upon to give profitable results in Colorado."

It will be noticed in the table that Early Paris and Early London, two varieties which have long been popular at the East, entirely failed to head.

Variety.	Seed from	Heads Mature	Remarks.
Early Snowball.	Henderson.	July 20.	Heads compact, very white, leaves smaller, very uniform.
Extra E. Erfurt.	Henderson.	Aug. 6.	Heads fairly solid and white, leaves large.
Extra Early Paris.	Landreth.	Aug. 24.	Heads solid and white, leaves very large.
Early Paris.	Ferry.	......	No heads formed.
Early Snowball.	Landreth.	Aug. 6.	Heads compact, very white, plant dwarf, small leaves.
Gerry Island.	Gregory.	......	No heads formed.
Select Dwarf Erfurt.	Landreth.	July 24.	Heads large and compact, very white and uniform.
Burpee's Earliest.	Burpee.	July 30.	Heads compact and white, leaves large.
Lenormand.	Landreth.	Sept. 20.	Heads solid and white, plant vigorous and dwarf.
Long Isl'd Beauty.	Low.	Aug. 24.	Heads loose, yellowish white, inferior stock.
Algiers.	Landreth.	Oct. 10.	Heads solid and large, plant vigorous, leaves very large.
Walcheren.	Landreth.	......	No heads formed.
Large L. Dutch.	Landreth.	Oct. 10.	Heads fairly compact, plant vigorous & large.
Late London.	Ferry.	......	No heads formed.
Landreth's First.	Landreth.	Aug. 21.	Heads solid, very white, of superior quality.
Vick's Ideal.	Low.	Aug. 6.	Heads solid, yellowish white, leaves large.

MICHIGAN EXPERIMENT STATION (*Lansing*).—The
Michigan experiment station is connected with the
Agricultural College, located at Lansing, at the
geographical centre of the Lower Peninsula. It
is, therefore, remote from any large body of water,
and although the soil in that portion of the state is
mainly a strong loam suitable for cauliflower, it is
only in favorable seasons that good cauliflowers can
be obtained.

In the exceptionally favorable season of 1889,
some of the sorts then prominently before the public, were grown at the college, all of which gave
very good results, with the exception of Autumn
Giant, which failed to germinate. The American
grown seeds, from H. A. March, of Fidalgo, Washington, were large and plump and gave strong vigorous plants, and as good or better results than is
usually obtained from imported seed. The following varieties were sown March 13, and set out May
14. It was difficult to detect any difference between Puritan, Gilt Edge, Denmark, Prize Earliest,
Best Early, Snowball, and Erfurt, as they showed
less variation than appeared between the same sorts
from different seedsmen.

The title "edible maturity" in the table refers to
the period at which the heads might be cut for
one's own use, that is when they had attained the
size of one's two fists. "Marketable maturity" is
when they had completed their growth and would
remain solid no longer.

12

Varieties.	Source.	Appearance of young plants, March 29.	Edible Maturity.	Mark't'ble Maturity.	Per cent. forming heads.
Burpee's Best Early	Burpee.	Small; even.	Aug. 5	Aug. 10	100
Denmark	Vaughn.	Good; even.	July 26	Aug. 10	83
Earliest Dwarf Erfurt	Maule.	Good; even.	Aug. 27	Sept. 14	67
Erfurt Earliest Dwarf	March.	Small; even.	Aug. 10	Aug. 27	92
Early Snowball	Henderson.	Very weak; uneven.	Aug. 5	Aug. 10	100
Early Puritan	Ferry.	Small; even.	Aug. 7	Aug. 13	92
Gilt Edge	Thorburn.	Weak; uneven.	July 26	Aug. 8	83
Maule's Prize Earliest	Maule.	Small; somewhat uneven.	July 21	Aug. 8	83
Snowball	March.	Good; even.	July 24	Aug. 8	100

THE BEST VARIETIES.

The points to consider in selecting varieties are first, earliness or time of maturity; second, the certainty of their forming good heads. The importance of having well grown seed has already been mentioned. This being secured, the choice of varieties is largely a matter of circumstances. A variety which is good for one climate, or for one purpose; may not be good for another. For the early crop, an account of which has already been given, the earliest variety obtainable should be used, as our springs at the North are short enough at best. The Earliest Dwarf Erfurt strains include nearly all the earliest varieties now grown, and, for this country, at least, are the best. The typical variety is usually sold under the name Extra Early Dwarf Erfurt, and if properly selected seed is secured, this is nearly or quite as early as any of the strains which have received special names. Among the best of these latter are Henderson's Snowball, Thorburn's Gilt Edge, and Vick's Ideal, the latter a little the largest and latest. For growing under glass the first two of these varieties are as good as any. The earliest varieties are now often grown also for the fall crop, particularly at the North, by being sown late. Their greater certainty to head on time, and the increased number that can be grown on an acre, renders them especially valuable.

A variety which in the past has given the most general satisfaction for the fall crop is Early Paris. Of the later maturing varieties, Veitch's Autumn Giant and Lenormand Short-stem, have been, and are still, popular, especially at the South. At present probably more than three fourths of the cauliflowers grown in this country are of the new varieties of the Dwarf Erfurt group. For the North, especially, these are now the most reliable and are increasing in popularity.

CHAPTER IX

BROCCOLI.

The Broccolis are so similar to the cauliflowers that some account of them may be expected in a treatise on the latter vegetable. In fact, no important structural difference between the two vegetables exists, the broccolis being merely a more robust and hardy group of varieties, requiring a longer period for development, and adapted, in mild climates, to cultivation during the winter. They are, in fact, often called "winter cauliflowers." They receive but little attention in the United States, where the winters, at least at the north, in the vicinity of the leading markets, are too severe for the out-door growth of vegetables of any kind. For this reason cauliflowers, which come to maturity in a single season, are grown instead. The supply of these two vegetables, therefore, which in western Europe, by means of successive sowings of varieties of both cauliflowers and broccolis, may be maintained the year round, is here, owing to the conditions of our climate, confined chiefly to the seasons of the year in which cauliflower can be obtained.

Although no sharp distinctions can be drawn between broccolis and cauliflowers, there are cer-

tain general differences which separate them.
As has been said, the broccolis are all of them
hardier than the cauliflowers, and require a
longer time in which to develop, so that in climates
having mild winters they are usually treated as
biennials. In France, the seed which is sown
about the first of May gives plants which head the
following spring before the early cauliflowers come
in. The plants are sometimes enabled to pass the
winter more safely by being taken up and planted
again in a slanting position.

In the appearance of the heads no difference
exists between cauliflowers and broccolis, except
that the latter are usually smaller, less compact,
and sometimes purple or sulphur colored. All
cauliflowers (with one or two exceptions), have
white compact heads. The stems of the broccolis
are usually taller than those of cauliflowers, the
leaves more numerous, larger, stiffer, but more
undulated, more rounded at the apex, and more frequently having a distinct stem or petiole. The mid-
ribs and principal veins are large and white, except
in varieties having colored heads, when they have
the same color as the head. The color of the leaves
is always more glaucous, that is, of a darker and
more bluish green, than is usual in the cauliflowers.

Broccolis, especially the colored varieties, are
sometimes said to be more tender in texture and

finer in flavor than the cauliflowers. This, however, is due only to the fact that they usually head in cool weather. When grown under the same conditions the cauliflowers are milder than the broccolis, and although to some tastes the more pronounced flavor of the latter may be preferred, most persons use broccoli only because in the winter season fresh cauliflowers cannot be obtained.

Nearly every one prefers cauliflower to broccoli, and the mild white varieties to the colored varieties of the latter vegetable. Broccolis sometimes acquire a bitter taste, the cause of which is not known. The methods of using the two vegetables are the same, except that the branching or sprouting broccolis are also cooked like asparagus.

The early history of the broccoli has already been treated in connection with that of the cauliflower.

The number of varieties of broccoli in cultivation is probably somewhat less than those of the cauliflower, but the differences between the varieties themselves are greater. Messrs. Sutton & Sons, of Reading, England, catalogue thirty-six varieties of broccoli and only eleven of cauliflower. Most of these varieties originated in England, where broccoli is more largely grown than anywhere else. Two groups of broccolis may be recognized, the "sprouting broccolis," which do not form compact heads, and the improved varieties with well formed heads, known as "cauliflower broccolis." The latter differ but little in any way from true cauliflowers.

The requirements of cultivation for the broccolis are practically the same as those for cauliflowers. Their value depends mainly on their greater hardiness, and on this account they are likely, at the South where the winters are mild enough, to become more extensively cultivated. They do not, however, endure hot weather as well as cauliflowers, and on this account it is doubtful if they ever become as largely grown anywhere in this country as they are in England.

The question of protecting them in winter, and the amount and kind of protection needed, depend of course on the severity of the winters. In Northern Florida, where cauliflowers are liable to be killed during winter, broccolis will stand out without any protection. In localities where but little protection is required, it may be afforded by loosening the roots and turning the plants down upon their sides. If more protection is needed they may be taken up and set in trenches and partly covered with straw and boards. Broccolis stand shipment better than cauliflowers. This is not only because they are generally handled in colder weather, but because they are somewhat coarser and firmer in texture. They do not sell for quite so good a price as cauliflowers. There are seven varieties catalogued by American seedsmen, of which the Early Purple Cape is the best adapted to our climate.

CHAPTER X.

COOKING CAULIFLOWER.

"Of all the flowers in the garden, I like the Cauliflower best."   DR. SAMUEL JOHNSON.

Dr. Johnson appreciated good living, and therefore it is not surprising that he should have left on record this tribute to the most delicate and finely flavored of all the cabbage family.

Cauliflower is so rarely seen in market in the United States, except in large cities, that comparatively few of our people are accustomed to using it. On this account a variety of receipts for cooking cauliflower are here given, in order to make the methods of using this excellent vegetable more widely known. Americans, especially, need to become familiar with its use; for to the English, French, and Germans, who have known it in the Old World, it needs no introduction.

Cauliflower lends itself readily to both plain and fancy methods of cooking. It is easy of digestion, and is an especial favorite with those who, from any reason, are unable to readily digest cabbage. Besides, it is more nutritious than the cabbage, and it is not exceeded in this particular by any other garden vegetable.

The following tables show the comparative composition of fresh cabbage and cauliflower, and the
composition of the ash of the latter. It will be
noticed that the percentage of ash and indigestible
fibre is low in the cauliflower, and the amount of
nitrogenous and starchy matter high.

ANALYSIS OF CABBAGE' AND CAULIFLOWER.

(König's Nohrungsmittel. pp. 715, 717).

	Cabbage.	Cauliflower.
Water....................	89.97	90.87
Nitrogenous bodies........	1.89	2.48
Fat.....................	0.20	0.34
Sugar....................	2.29	1.21
Nitrogen free extract (starch, dextrine, etc.)....	2.58	3.34
Fiber...................	1.84	0 91
Ash....................	1.23	0.83

ANALYSIS OF CAULIFLOWER ASH.

(Whitner's Gardening in Florida).

Potassa...	34.39
Soda	14.79
Lime	2 96
Magnesia..	2.38
Sulphuric Acid..............................	11.16
Silicic Acid......................	1.92
Phosphoric Acid............................	25.87
Phosphate of Iron..........................	3.67
Chloride of Sodium........................	2.78

Cauliflower is not wholly free from the odor which renders the cooking of cabbage so unpleasant, but in this respect it is much less objectionable than cabbage. As with cabbage, this odor is in some cases more marked than in others, depending on the character of the soil, and the quantity and nature of the manure used. A small piece of red pepper added to the water in which cauliflower or cabbage is boiled prevents to a large extent this unpleasant odor and improves their flavor. To obviate the "strong" flavor which these vegetables acquire when large quantities of stable manure are used the heads should be parboiled in the morning of the day on which they are wanted. They are then put on a hair sieve and placed in the larder. Twenty minutes before they are wanted for the table they are to be reboiled steadily until the strong taste is gone.

When cauliflowers are preserved in a shed or cellar they often become more or less wilted and strong in flavor, and can then be rendered palatable only by cutting them off from the stalks on the previous day and throwing them into cold, salted water, frequently changing it until they are wanted; in this way the heads become plumped up, and the strong disagreeable smell and taste which they have acquired is in some degree removed; but even under the most careful treatment they lose their fine, white cauliflower color.

To remove any caterpillars or other insects which may have found lodgment in the cauliflower head it should be examined as carefully as possible, opening it a little if necessary. It should then be placed top down in cold salt water for an hour; or, better still, in cold water and vinegar. This is believed to be particularly effective in dislodging any insect life that may be present. If the heads seem badly infested, however, which they seldom are, the only safe way is to break them up before cooking.

In cooking the heads whole, which is a favorite method, care is needed not to boil too long, so as to cause the head to come to pieces. To prevent any danger of breaking the head in cooking, it should be wrapped in cheese cloth or other similar material, in which it is to be handled.

Cauliflower is in season in this country from June until December, but is most abundant during the month of October. Those found in market during the hottest summer months are apt to be dark in color, somewhat strong in flavor, and filled with small leaves. Broccoli is cooked in nearly all cases precisely as cauliflower.

Porcelain lined or similarly guarded pots should be used in which to cook these vegetables, as iron is liable to impart to them a dark color.

The use of earthenware vessels in which to cook vegetables of the cabbage tribe is recommended as follows by a writer in the *American Garden*:

"To have any of the Brassicæ in proper flavor
we must go to the German housewives and learn of
them to cook cabbage, cauliflower, etc., in earthenware instead of metal. The German potters make
stout boilers, like huge bean-pots, that hold six or
eight cabbages, for restaurant cooking, and they
are quite a different vegetable treated in this way.
Try the experiment; put a cabbage in a stone jar
with plenty of water, cover tight and boil till tender.
I think it does not take as long to cook in this way
as in ordinary kettles, the steady mild heat soften-
ing the tissues more steadily than the open boiling.
And there is little or no smell to cabbage or onions
cooked in a close stone pot in the oven. A cabbage
baked in its own steam in such a pot and served
with hot vinegar and butter is a high-flavored
dish."

A writer in the *Rural New Yorker* sums up the
prime requirements in cooking cauliflower as follows:

"Four rules never to be deviated from may be
laid down: first, that the cauliflower is to be soaked
in salt and water for at least a half hour before
cooking, in order to drive out any insects or worms
that may be lurking among the flowerets; second,
(if to be boiled) when ready for cooking the vegetable is to be plunged into salted, thoroughly boiling water; third, it is not to be cooked a moment

after it becomes tender; fourth, to be served as soon as done. Neglect of any of these points is sure to result in failure, while a careful following of them will give a wholesome, delicate dish, and one that will be eaten with gusto and remembered with pleasure."

A very simple method of serving cauliflower is with milk and butter, after the manner of cabbage, but a more elaborate white sauce generally accompanies it. This is the familiar drawn butter sauce, to which may be added a little vinegar or lemon juice, to give piquancy of flavor. Sometimes this sauce is varied by adding milk or cream to the flour and butter, when it is called "cream sauce."

The receipts given below are chiefly from the following four recent works on cookery:

"Good Living," by Sara Van Buren Brugière; G. P. Putnam's Sons, New York and London, 1890.

"The Buckeye Cook-Book"; Buckeye Publishing Company, Minneapolis, 1887.

"Our Home Cyclopedia," by Edgar S. Darling; Mercantile Publishing Company, Detroit, 1889

"Mrs. A. B. Marshall's Cookery Book"; Marshall's School of Cookery, London, 1888.

1. BOILED (*Gardener's Text.Book*).—The head should be cut with most of the surrounding leaves attached, which are to be trimmed off when the time comes for cooking. Let it lie half an hour in

salt and water, and then boil it in fresh water for fifteen or twenty minutes, until a fork will easily enter the stem. Milk and water are better than water alone [a little sweet milk tends to keep the heads white]. Serve with sauce, gravy or melted butter.

2. BOILED (*American Agriculturist*).—Boil in water, slightly salted--never with meat. When tender, which will usually be with twenty minutes cooking, take up and drain and cover with drawn butter (white sauce, made with butter, flour and water) and serve hot. They are usually eaten without other addition, but some dress with pepper and vinegar--the same as they do cabbage.

3. BOILED (*Good Living*).—Trim off the outside leaves, leaving one row around the flower. Cut an X in the stalk. Have a large pot of boiling water on the fire. Add enough milk to whiten the water; also one level teaspoonful of salt. The cauliflower should be left in vinegar and water for twenty to thirty minutes before boiling. This system is supposed to draw out any insects that may lurk within. Drain it thoroughly; tie it loosely in a piece of cheese-cloth large enough to cover it entirely. Put it into the boiling water, which must cover it well. Let it boil until quite tender, but be careful that it does not go to pieces. As cauliflowers vary very much in size, only a general idea of the time re-

13

quired can be given.   One of ordinary size will take
about forty minutes, perhaps more.   When cooked
lift it out by the cheese-cloth, drain very thoroughly,
and set in a round dish.   Make a cream sauce
(No. 42), pour it over the cauliflower, cover, and
let it stand for a few minutes for the sauce to penetrate.   Then serve.   *Or*, if a handsome specimen
successfully boiled, serve it in a round dish with a
white sauce (No. 41) served separately in a sauce-
boat.   Add a squeeze of lemon juice to the sauce
before serving.   Small cauliflowers will not require
more than thirty minutes to boil.

4. BOILED (*Buckeye Cook Book*).—To each two
quarts of water allow a heaping teaspoon of salt;
choose close and white cauliflower; trim off decayed
outside leaves, and cut stock off flat at bottom.
Open flower a little in places to remove insects,
which are generally found around the stalk, and
let cauliflowers lie with head downward in salt and
water for two hours previous to dressing them,
which will effectually draw out all vermin.   Then
put in boiling water, adding salt in above proportion, and boil briskly for fifteen or twenty minutes
over a good fire, keeping saucepan uncovered.
Water should be well skimmed, and when cauliflowers are tender, take up, drain, and if large
enough, place upright in a dish; serve with plain
melted butter, a little of which may be poured over

the flowers; or a white sauce may be used, made as follows: Put butter size of an egg into saucepan, and when it bubbles stir in a scant half teacup of flour; stir well with an egg-whisk until cooked; then add two teacups of thin cream, some pepper and salt. Stir it over the fire until perfectly smooth. Pour the sauce over the cauliflower and serve. Many let the cauliflower simmer in the same sauce a few moments before serving.

Cauliflower is delicious served as a garnish around spring chicken, or with fried sweet-breads, when the white sauce should be poured over both. In this case it should be made by adding the cream, flour and seasoning to the little grease (half a teaspoon) that is left after frying the chickens or sweet-breads.

5. BAKED (*Buckeye Cook Book*).—Prepare as for boiling, and parboil five minutes; cut into pieces and put into a pie dish; add a little milk, season with salt, pepper and butter; cover with dry, grated cheese, and bake.

6. STEAMED (*Mrs. M. P. A. Crozier*).—Lay the nicely prepared cauliflower head in the deep dish from which it is to be served at table, sprinkle salt over it, place it in the steamer, cover closely, and steam till tender. Remove to the table, and pour over it rich, sweet cream, slightly salted and heated.

7. STEWED (*Gardener's Chronicle*).— Cut up your cauliflower into sprigs of convenient size to serve with a tablespoon, and throw them into cold water an hour before cooking. To stew them, have a stout, iron stewpan, white-enamelled inside—an ordinary tin saucepan or boiler will hardly do. Put a large lump of butter into your stewpan as you set it over a gentle fire; instead of butter you may use the fat taken from the top of cold roast meat gravy—that of beef or veal is preferable to that of mutton. As the grease melts, stir into it an onion chopped very fine, and a little flour and water; continue stirring until the whole is nicely browned; then put in your sprigged cauliflower, adding only just enough water or broth to cook it; season lightly with pepper and salt, and a very light dust of grated nutmeg, if not disapproved; let it stew gently till perfectly tender; when done the gravy should be so reduced as to be no more in quantity than is wanted to serve as sauce with the vegetable; for this reason the salt must be used with great moderation, otherwise, by concentration, the gravy would be converted into brine; transfer the cauliflower from the stewpan to a hot dish, and pour the reduced gravy over it.

Note that by this method nothing is lost. The natural and nutritive juices of the vegetable, the sugar and albumen, are retained instead of being drawn out and diluted by boiling in several pints of water, and consequently wasted and thrown away. Note also that this receipt is founded (like the directions for many other good dishes) on the *roux*—flour browned in butter—which is one of the grand elements in French cookery.

8. STEWED (*Mr. S. J. Soyer**).—Cauliflower butter, salt, sugar, two and one-third ounces of flour, half a pint of cream, one-eighth of the soup from the cauliflower.

The cauliflower is cut into pieces, boiled slightly in salted water, taken out of the soup and put on a colander to drain. The butter and flour are baked together and thinned with the cream, and about the quantity of the soup above stated. The cauliflower is put into this sauce and again brought to a boil, whereupon it is served warm.

9. ESCALLOPED (*Rural New Yorker*).—Place a layer of the parboiled flowerets in a pudding dish, and cover them with cream sauce enough to moisten, with the addition of a little grated cheese, usually Parmesian; this is to be followed by another layer of this vegetable, and the whole covered with bread crumbs dotted with bits of butter.

10. ESCALLOPED (*Buckeye Cook Book*).—Boil till tender, drain well, and cut in small pieces; put in

---

* Chief Cook at the Court of Denmark.

layers, with fine chopped egg, and this dressing: Half pint milk, thickened over boiling water. with two tablespoons flour and seasoned with two tea-spoons salt, one of white pepper and two table-spoons butter; put grated bread over the top: dot it with small bits of butter and place it in the oven to heat thoroughly and brown. Serve in same dish in which it was baked. This is a good way to use common heads.

A nicer way is to boil them. then place them whole in a buttered dish with stems down. Make sauce with a cup of bread crumbs beaten to froth with two tablespoons melted butter and three of cream or milk. one well-beaten egg, and salt and pep-per to taste. Pour this over the cauliflower. cover dish tightly, and bake six minutes in a quick oven. browning them nicely. Serve as above.

11. WITH STUFFING (*Home Cyclopedia*). Take a saucepan, the exact size of the dish in-tended to be used. Cleanse a large, firm, white cauliflower, and cut into sprigs. throw those into boiling salt water for two minutes; then take them out, drain, and pack them tightly with the heads downwards, in the saucepan, the bottom of which must have been previously covered with thin slices of bacon; fill up the vacant spaces with a stuffing made of three tablespoonfuls of finely minced veal, the same of beef suet, four tablespoonfuls of

bread crumbs. a little pepper and salt, a teaspoonful of chopped parsley, a teaspoonful of minced chives and a dozen small mushrooms, chopped fine. Strew these ingredients over the cauliflowers in alternate layers and pour over them three well-beaten eggs. When these are well soaked add sufficient nicely-flavored stock to cover the whole; simmer gently till the cauliflowers are tender, and the sauce very much reduced; then turn the contents of the saucepan upside down on a hot dish, and the cauliflowers will be found standing in a savory mixture.

12. WITH SAUCE (*Home Cyclopedia*).—Boil a large cauliflower—tied in netting—in hot salted water, from twenty-five to thirty minutes; drain, serve in a deep dish with the flower upwards, and pour over it a cup of drawn butter in which has been stirred the juice of a lemon and a half teaspoonful of French mustard, mixed up well with the sauce.

13. WITH CURRY SAUCE (*Mrs. Marshall*).—Blanch (see note to No. 19) and plain boil the cauliflower for fifteen to twenty minutes till tender, then cut it up into nice long pieces, each sufficient for one person; place the pieces in a saute pan and pour the curry sauce (as for curry *à la simla*) over them; let it boil up, and then draw the pan to the side of the stove and let it stay there for ten or twelve

minutes; dish the pieces up in the form of cutlets, pour the sauce over them, and garnish round the cauliflower with little bunches of grated cocoanut which have been warmed between two plates over boiling water. This is an excellent dish for luncheon or second course, or it may be served in place of an entrée.

14. WITH TOMATO SAUCE (*Good Living*).—Having boiled a medium-sized cauliflower, very carefully as directed (No. 3) place it on a round dish, after having thoroughly drained it. Have ready a rich tomato sauce (No. 40) pour it around (not over) the cauliflower, and serve as a separate course. This is a very pretty dish.

15. WITH TOMATO SAUCE (*Good Health*).—Boil or steam the cauliflower until tender. In another dish prepare a sauce by heating a pint of strained stewed tomatoes to boiling, thickening with a tablespoonful of flour, and salting to taste. When the cauliflower is tender, dish, and pour over it the hot tomato sauce.

16. WITH MUSHROOMS (*Buckeye Cook Book*).— Put in a frying pan, in hot fat, a few small mushrooms and part of a cauliflower, broken into sprigs. Sprinkle over them some grated cheese, and baste the whole well from time to time with the hot fat.

17. WITH BRUSSELS SPROUTS (*Mr. S. J. Soyer*).— Cauliflower, Brussels sprouts, dotter of egg, butter,

a tablespoonful of cream, half a pint of sauce for vegetables, potato puré—that is, bouillon thickened with mashed potatoes and strained.

Both cauliflower and sprouts are to be well cleaned, boiled separately in salt water and served on the puré, the cauliflower in the centre and the sprouts around it for garnishing. The sauce, to which is added the egg dotters, butter and cream, is poured hot over the cauliflower and sprouts.

18. Au Gratin (*Good Living*).—Boil the cauliflower as directed. Set it in a round baking dish which can be sent to the table. For a moderate sized cauliflower make one pint of cream sauce (No. 42). Add to the sauce two heaping tablespoons each or grated Parmesian and Gruyère cheese and a dash of cayenne. Mix the sauce and pour it over the cauliflower, letting it penetrate all the crevices. Cover the top with fine grated breadcrumbs, dot with butter, and bake twenty minutes. Serve in the same dish.

19. Au Gratin (*Mrs. Marshall*).—Trim the cauliflower and blanch it*; put it to boil in boiling water till it is tender; then take up and drain. Butter the dish on which it is to be served and put on it about two tablespoonfuls of the sauce as

* Blanching anything is placing it on the fire in cold water until it boils, and after straining it off plunging it into cold water for the purpose of rendering it white.

below (No. 39); put the cauliflower on the sauce, then cover it over thickly with sauce, and smooth it all over with a palette knife; sprinkle it with browned bread-crumbs; stand the dish in an ordinary baking tin containing about a pint of boiling water; place in the oven for about fifteen or twenty minutes, and when a nice golden color take it from the oven and sprinkle over it a very little grated Parmesian cheese. Stand the dish on another with a napkin, and serve very hot as a second course or luncheon dish.

20. AU GRATIN (*Mr. S. J. Soyer*).—Three cauliflower heads, salt, pepper, grated bread, two eggs, one-quarter pound grated Parmesian cheese, one-quarter pound grated Swiss cheese, one pint white sauce.

The cauliflowers are boiled rare, taken out and drained off. White sauce and spices are boiled thick and the egg dotters and cheese mixed with it. The cauliflowers are cut to pieces and put in layers with sauce between, on a dish or silver saucepan, are sprinkled with grated bread and cheese, put fifteen minutes into a hot oven to be browned with a salamander. Serve as an independent dish.

In place of " white sauce " butter and flour may be baked together and thinned with sweet milk.

21. CAULIFLOWER AU NATUREL (*Mr. J. S. Soyer*).— The stem of the white, solid cauliflower heads is cut

off an inch from the head, and with a penknife is cleaned of the hard outer membrane, taking care to preserve the head as whole as possible; the head is then well rinsed in cold water, to which is added some vinegar to drive out larvæ and the like; it is then boiled in salt water until it is tender, when it is taken up to drain off on a sieve or colander. It is to be served high on a napkin, with melted butter, common sauce for vegetables, Dutch sauce, *velouté* or *mâitre d'hôtel* sauce.

N. B.—For cauliflowers, and vegetables generally, the sauce ought to be rather thick, as it is impossible to have the vegetables run perfectly dry when they are to be served warm.

22. Á LA FRANCAISE (*Home Cyclopedia*).—After trimming properly, cut the cauliflower into quarters, and put into a stewpan and boil until tender; drain and arrange it neatly on a dish. Pour over it melted butter.

23. Á LA LOUIS XIV (*Mr. S. J. Soyer*).—Cauliflower, new-made butter, grated nutmeg, bouillon.

The cauliflower is to be repeatedly washed in lukewarm water, boiled with bouillon and a little nutmeg, drained and then shaken with butter over a fire. To be served as soon as the butter is melted.

24. A LA VARENNE (*Mrs. Marshall*).—Trim a cauliflower, and place it in salt and water for about

one hour; then put it into cold water with a pinch of salt; bring to the boil, and then rince the cauliflower and put it again into boiling water which is seasoned with salt, to cook till tender. When cooked, cut it in pieces and dish up in a coil; pour parsley sauce over, and garnish it round with braised carrots or a macedoine of vegetables, and place the cut up stalks of cauliflower in the centre. Serve for a luncheon or second course dish.

25. En Mayonaise (*Mr. S. J. Soyer*). — Two heads of cauliflower, salt, pepper, sweet oil, estragon, chopped parsley, vinegar, oil-sauce.

The cauliflowers are to be plucked apart and the stemlets cut off at proper lengths. Boil in water, and salt when nearly done. Drain off and let cool, and then marinate for an hour with oil, vinegar, spices, estragon and parsley. Drain on a sieve. To be served high on a dish, and oil sauce gradually to be poured over. If desired, the dish might be garnished with carrots or some other suitable vegetable.

26. Souffle of Cauliflower, À la Baronne (*Mrs. Marshall*).—Trim a nice cauliflower, put it to blanch (note to No. 19), then rince it and put it into boiling water with a little salt, and let it cook till tender; take up again, drain, and cut it in neat pieces and place them in a buttered souffle dish with alternate layers of raw sliced tomatoes; season

with a very little salt and white pepper, and fill up
the dish with a souffle mixture prepared as below,
and sprinkle over with a few browned bread
crumbs; place a few pieces of butter here and there
on the top, and bake in a moderate oven for thirty
minutes, dish upon a paper with a napkin round,
sprinkle it with a little chopped parsley, and serve
for second course or luncheon.

Mixture for Cauliflower Souffle. — Mix two
ounces of butter, one and a half ounces of fine
flour, one and a half raw yolks of eggs, tiny dust
of cayenne, a saltspoonful of salt, with not quite
half a pint of cold milk; stir over the fire till it
boils, then add three ounces of grated Parmesian
cheese and the whites of three eggs that have been
whipped stiff, with a pinch of salt, and use.

27. CAULIFLOWER SALAD (*Good Living*).—One pint
cold boiled cauliflower, one teaspoon of chervil,
chopped as fine as powder, one teaspoon of parsley,
chopped as fine as powder, one teaspoon of tarragon
or Maille vinegar, French dressing.

Boil the cauliflower as directed (No. 3). Separate the flowerets, mix with the parsley, chives and
dressing. Set aside one hour. Serve very cold.

Another (*Buckeye Cook Book*).—After boiling,
let cool and dress with Mayonnaise, or any dressing
preferred.

28. Cauliflower Omelette.—Take the white part of a boiled cauliflower after it is cold, chop it very small, and mix with it a sufficient quantity of well beaten egg to make a very thick batter; then fry it in fresh butter, in a small pan, and send to the table hot.

Note:—This omelette makes a fine dressing to pour hot over fried chicken when ready to send to the table.

29. Cauliflower Soup (*Mr. S. J. Soyer*). Two and a half quarts bouillon, one and a half pint milk, two or three cauliflowers, two and a half ounces butter, one and a half ounce flour, sugar, salt.

The cauliflowers are cleaned, and boiled almost ready, taken out and put on a sieve, and the soup preserved. The butter and flour are baked together; and with the milk, bouillon, sugar and salt added to the decoction from the cauliflowers. These are then cut into proper pieces and put into the soup, which is subjected to a quick boil and then served with bread dumplings: crumbs of white bread moistened with milk, melted butter, dotter of eggs, and the whites beaten to a stiff froth—the mass rolled into balls, and boiled until they float.

30. Cauliflower Cream Soup (*Rural New Yorker*).—Boil the cauliflower in salt water until nearly done. For a small head, bring another quart

of water (or milk and water) to boil, adding half an
onion, or a bit of spice if desired, and thicken it as
for drawn butter sauce, with an ounce of butter
and some flour. Boil the cauliflower in the liquid
until soft, then put the whole through a colander;
return to the fire, and add a cup of cream; simmer
for five minutes, and serve at once, with squares of
fried bread.

31. BROCCOLI (*American Garden*).—Broccoli is
a pleasant change from cabbage and cauliflower,
either as a salad or a side dish. To dress it, strip
off the little branches, till the top one is left, then
with a sharp knife peel off all the hard skin on the
stalks and branchlets and throw them into water.
When the water in the stewpan boils, put in the
broccoli and cook till tender, salting in the last
five minutes. Serve with toast dipped in the broccoli water, laying the stalks over it, and eat with
vinegar and melted butter. Or, let it get cold, cut
in small bits, and serve as salad with oil and vinegar, with lemon juice, garnished with nasturtium
buds. Or, serve a large round of toast, the size of
a dinner plate, moistened with broccoli water,
salted and buttered, with nicely poached eggs laid
on it, and sprigs of hot broccoli set thickly between,
dusting with fine salt. Cauliflower and solid white
cabbage may be served the same way.

32. Egg Broccoli (*Home Cyclopedia*). — Take half a dozen heads of broccoli, cut off the small shoots or blossoms and lay them aside for frying; trim the stalks short and pare off the rough rind up to the head, wash them well and lay them in salt water for an hour, then put them into plenty of boiling water (salted) and let them boil fast till quite tender. Put two ounces of butter into a saucepan, and stir it over a slow fire till it is melted; then add gradually six or eight well-beaten eggs and stir the mixture until it is thick and smooth. Lay the broccoli in the center of a large dish, pour the egg around it, and, having firied the broccoli blossoms, arrange them in a circle near the edge of the dish.

33. Pickled (*Mrs. M. P. A. Crozier*).—Break at the natural divisions, steam till tender, and place in a jar of cold vinegar with mustard and red peppers.

34. Pickled (*Gardener's Text Book*).—Place the heads in a keg, and sprinkle them liberally with salt. Let them remain thus for about a week, when you may turn over them scalding hot vinegar, prepared with one ounce of mace, one ounce of pepper-corns, and one ounce of cloves to every gallon. Draw off the vinegar, and return it scalding hot several times until the heads become tender.

35. Pickled (*Rural New Yorker*).—Break the heads into small sprays, throw them into a kettle

of scalding brine; let them come to a boil, and drain carefully, so as not to break them; pack in stone or glass jars, and cover with scalding vinegar seasoned as follows: To one gallon of vinegar allow one cup of white sugar, half an ounce of mace, one ounce of peppercorns, two or three red pepper pods broken into bits, and a tablespoonful each of coriander seed, celery seed, and white mustard. Pour this hot over the cauliflowers and seal at once. Glass jars are the most convenient, as they may be examined frequently to see if their contents are keeping well. If not, repeat the scalding. In all pickles the vinegar should be two inches or more above the vegetables, as it is sure to shrink, and if the vegetables are not thoroughly immersed in vinegar they will not keep.

36. PICKLED (*Home Cyclopedia*).—Choose such as are firm, yet of their full size; cut away all the leaves and pare the stalks; pull away the flowers in bunches, steep in brine two days, then drain them, wipe them dry, and put them in hot pickle, or merely infuse for three days three ounces of curry powder in every quart of vinegar.

Another. Slice, salt for two or three days, drain, spread upon a dry cloth before the fire twenty-four hours; put in a jar and cover with spiced vinegar.

37. MIXED PICKLES (*Home Cyclopedia*).—Three hundred small cucumbers, four green peppers

14

sliced fine, two large or three small heads of cauliflower, three heads of white cabbage sliced fine, nine large onions sliced, one large horseradish, one quart green beans cut one inch long, one quart green tomatoes sliced; put this mixture in a pretty strong brine twenty-four hours; drain three hours; then sprinkle in one-fourth pound black and one-fourth pound white mustard seed; also one tablespoonful black ground pepper; let it come to a boil in just vinegar enough to cover it, adding a little alumn; drain again, and when cold put in one-half pint ground mustard; cover the whole with good cider vinegar; add turmeric enough to color if you like.

ACCESSORY RECEIPTS.

38. CAULIFLOWER SAUCE (*Good Living*).—Use either white or cream sauce, adding to it the flowerets of cauliflower previously boiled tender. Serve with boiled fowl, veal sauté, etc.

39. CAULIFLOWER SAUCE (*To accompany No. 19*).—One pint of thick Bechamel sauce, a quarter of a pound of grated Parmesian cheese, two tablespoonfuls of grated Gruyère cheese, two tablespoonfuls of cream, a little dust of cayenne pepper and a pinch of salt; mix well together, and use.

40. TOMATO SAUCE (*To accompany No 14*).—

6 large tomatoes, or 1 can,	2 chopped onions,
Butter, size of an egg,	Salt and pepper,
Bunch of parsley or thyme,	Pinch of sugar,
1 tablespoonful of butter,	2 tablespoonfuls of flour.

Peel the tomatoes, and put into a sauce pan with butter, thyme, onions and parsley (and 1 clove of garlic chopped and fried in butter). Set over boiling water and stew very gently for three hours. Then press fruit and juice all through a sieve, rejecting only the seeds and herbs. Meanwhile prepare a roux, allowing 1 quart of sauce, 1 tablespoonful of butter, and 2 of flour, stirred together over the fire until light golden brown—no darker, or the color of the sauce will be injured. When the sauce is strained, remove the roux from the fire; stir in the sauce. Return it to the fire. Stir and boil 3 to 5 minutes, until rich and thick. Should the sauce be already quite thick with the pulp of the tomatoes, use less thickening. If served with fricandeau, veal sauté, or filet of beef, add the juices of the meat to the sauce.

41.   WHITE SAUCE (*To accompany No. 3, etc.*)—

| 3 ounces of butter, | 1 ounce of flour, |
| 2 gills of water, | Pepper and salt. |

Put 2 ounces of the butter in a stew pan; when it melts, add the flour. Stir for 1 minute or more, but do not brown. Then add by degrees the boiling water, stirring until smooth; pass it through a sieve; then add the rest of the butter, cut in pieces. When the butter is melted, serve immediately. This makes about one pint of sauce. You may add as a great improvement a little lemon juice or a few drops of vinegar.

N. B.—If the sauce is to have other ingredients added it is best to have it very thick to begin with.

42.   CREAM SAUCE (*To accompany Nos. 3 and 18*).

1 tablespoon of flour	2 gills of new milk,
1 very large tablespoon of butter.	½ teaspoon of salt.

Pepper to taste.

Put ¾ of the butter in a sauce pan over the fire. As soon as it melts, add the flour; stir till blended. Be careful not to let it brown. Add the boiling milk, by degrees, to the flour and butter, stirring without ceasing. Boil 3 minutes. Remove from the fire; add salt, white pepper, and the rest of the butter; stir until the butter melts, and serve immediately. If it has to be kept, set it over a kettle of boiling water; leave the spoon in it, and every now and again stir it down or the top will form a scum. Do not let it boil after the last butter is added. Cream may be used instead of new milk.

RECAPITULATION.

The following recapitulation of the more important points connected with cauliflower culture will serve to fix them in mind:

1. The best localities for cauliflower growing are where the climate is cool and moist, as near some large body of water.

2. The cauliflower will stand nearly as much dry weather as ordinary crops while growing, providing it has a cool, moist time in which to head.

3. The best soil is a sandy loam, though any cool, moist, strong, fertile soil will answer.

4. While a cool, moist soil is desirable, thorough drainage is quite as essential as with any other crop.

5. An abundance of strong barnyard or other manure is necessary, as the cauliflower is a gross feeder.

6. Deep and frequent tillage, that there may be no check in growth until the plants are nearly ready to head.

7. Tie or pin the leaves over the heads as soon as they appear, to keep them blanched and protect them from frost.

8. If any plants have failed to head on the approach of winter, remove them to a shed or cellar, and they will head there.

9. Guard against the flea beetle, cut worm, cabbage worm and cabbage maggot in the same manner as with cabbage.

10. With suitable varieties and proper care the cauliflower can generally be successfully grown wherever the cabbage thrives particularly well.

GLOSSARY.

BLIND.—To " go blind " is to lose the centre or growing point, and fail to head. It is generally due to climatic or insect injury. It is said to be frequently caused in the cauliflower by an insect resembling the turnip fly. Soot and lime are remedies.

BLUES.—A dark-bluish appearance, accompanying arrested development, generally due to unfavorable weather, unsuitable soil or insects at the root. Cabbage and cauliflower plants which are set too early in the spring, especially if they are not well hardened off and are placed in a cold soil, are apt to assume this appearance. If cauliflowers remain long in this condition, they are liable either to fail to head, or to form small heads prematurely.

BOLT.—A familiar term in England, applied to wheat when it heads out small and prematurely. Sometimes applied to cauliflowers when they head before they attain a proper age and size. See *Button*.

BREAK.—To become loose or " frothy " preparatory to running up to seed. Said of a head of cauliflower; also of other plants as they begin to throw up their seed stalks.

Button.—To form small heads prematurely, as often occurs when plants are left too long in the seed-bed.

Curd.—The material composing the head of a cauliflower. Sometimes the heads individually are called "curds."

Drawn.—Having an abnormally long stem, owing to crowding, or too great heat, or too little light in the seed-bed.

Flower or Blossom.—Terms often applied to the head in the cauliflower, either from its resemblance to a flower, or from a mistaken idea that it really is a flower.

Floweret.—A term sometimes applied to one of the sprays or sub-divisions of a cauliflower head.

Frothy, see *Warty*.

Glaucous.—Pale bluish-green; sea-green.

Head.—The edible part of a cauliflower, consisting of a mass of thickened flower-stems at an early stage of growth, before they have separated and elongated preparatory to forming flowers and seeds. Various other terms have been applied to it, such as "flower" or "blossom," "boquet," "heart," and, by the French, "pomme" (apple), but sometimes also "tête" (head).

Heart, see *Head*.

Leafy.—Having the head interspersed with rather small leaves. A tendency to this condition is found in some inferior varieties, and in many good varieties when they head in hot weather.

Mossy.—Having numerous minute leaves distributed over the head, giving it a "mossy" appearance. It is a condition of the same nature as the "leafy" state above mentioned, and produced by the same causes.

Rogue.—An undesirable sport. A cauliflower which, unlike the others in the field, runs immediately to seed without forming a head, would be called a "rogue."

Running.—Throwing up the flower-stalks preparatory to the production of seed. See *Break*.

Turning In.—Commencing to head; a term originally applied to cabbages, but now extended to other plants which form heads of any kind.

Warty or Frothy.—A condition of the head in which the surface is covered with small prominences preparatory to running up to seed.

Weather-Proud.—An English term which signifies that plants are larger or more thrifty than proper for the time of year. Applied, for example, to wintered-over cauliflower plants during a warm, early spring.

REFERENCES.

In the following works and articles certain points in connection with the cauliflower and its cultivation are more fully treated than in the present work.

Bon Jardenier, (1859, p. 449).—A good article on the origin and varieties of the cauliflower, and its cultivation in France.

Brill, Francis.—"Cauliflowers and How to Grow Them," (16 pp., price twenty cents. Published by the Author, Riverhead, N. Y., 1886). A well written account of cauliflower growing on Long Island and the methods used.

Burpee, W. A.—"How to Grow Cabbages and Cauliflowers," (W. A. Burpee & Co., Philadelphia, 1890). A pamphlet of eighty-five pages, price thirty cents, consisting of prize essays on the Cabbage and Cauliflower, by Mr. G. H. Howard, of Long Island, N. Y., and Mr. J. Pedersen, of Denmark; together with directions for cooking these vegetables by Mr. S. J. Soyer, chief cook at the Court of Denmark; and a chapter on varieties by W. A. Burpee.

De Candolle, Augustin Pyramus.—" Memoir on the Different Species, Races and Varieties of the

Genus Brassica, and of the Genera Allied with It which are Cultivated in Europe" (read in 1821).— *Transactions of the Horticultural Society of London*, Vol. V, p. 1.

Don, Geo.—"General History of Dichlamydeous Plants," (4 volumes, London, 1831). Volume I, pp. 233–241, contains a good account of the culture and varieties of broccoli and cauliflower. Fifteen varieties of broccoli and three of cauliflower are described.

Journal of Horticulture and Cottage Gardener, (1878, p. 61).—A good article on the cultivation of cauliflower in England.

Loudon, J. C.—"Encyclopædia of Gardening" (5th edition, London, 1827). This standard work contains a very full account of the cauliflower and its allies, including quotations from various English authorities.

Magazine of Horticulture, (1839, p. 53).—A good article on the cultivation of the cauliflower in England.

Maher, John.—"Hints relative to the Culture of the Early Purple Broccoli" (read in 1808).— *Transactions of the Horticultural Society of London*, Vol. I, pp. 116–120. An account of the culture and varieties of broccoli, with remarks on its improvement, and on the liability of broccoli and cauliflower to mix with cabbage.

McIntosh, Charles.—"Book of the Garden" (2 volumes, London, 1853). The second volume contains the best account of cauliflower cultivation in England written up to that time.

Rogers, John.— "The Vegetable Cultivator" (London, 1843). Contains a good account of the cauliflower and the methods of growing it in England.

Sturtevant, Dr. E. L.—In his "History of Garden Vegetables," in the *American Naturalist,* this author gives the history of cauliflower and broccoli, including the earliest recorded evidences of their cultivation, and the names applied to these vegetables in different countries. The broccoli is treated in the volume for 1887, p. 438, and the cauliflower in the same volume, p. 701.

Sutton & Sons, Reading, England. — These seedsmen publish a work on Gardening, price five shillings, in which the subject of cauliflower culture in England is fully treated.

Vilmorin–Andrieux, et cie.—"*Plantes Potagers*" (Paris, 1883). This work by Vilmorin, Andrieux & Co., the Paris seedsmen, was translated into English, and published under the title of "The Vegetable Garden," by Murray, of London, in 1885. It contains full descriptions of varieties of cauliflower, based on trials at the experiment grounds of this firm at Paris, and also includes information on the cultivation of this vegetable in France.

INDEX.

www.ingramcontent.com/pod-product-compliance
Lightning Source LLC
Chambersburg PA
CBHW030106030726
47498CB00007B/2265